ONE IN A MILLION

ONE IN A MILLION

HARSHITA SRIVASTAVA

Published by
MAHAVEER PUBLISHERS
4764/2A, 23-Ansari Road, Daryaganj
New Delhi – 110002
Ph. : 011 – 66629669–79–89
e-mail : mahaveerpublishers@gmail.com

First Edition : May 2013

One In A Million
ISBN(10) : 9350880369
ISBN(13) : 9789350880364

Distributed in India by
VAIBHAV BOOK SERVICE
e-mail : vaibhavbookservice@gmail.com

Distributed in Nepal by
BAJRANGBALI BOOK ENTERPRISES PVT. LTD.
Jyatha Mushyabahal, Ward No. 27, Kathmandu, Nepal
e-mail : bajrangbalibooks@gmail.com

Printed in India

My father, Dr. R.P. Srivastava
Research Scientist, ICAR
and
My mother, Mrs. Mahima Srivastava
for bringing out the best in me

Acknowledgments

A book is never a one man's effort. It involves a whole lot of people to come in the final form. The book you are holding in your hand is my dream come true. And there are several people who need to be thanked for this.

To my Ma and Pa, Mrs. Mahima Srivastava and Dr. R.P. Srivastava for their never ending support and motivation. Without their belief in me, I would have never reached here. My younger sister needs special mention, life without you is tasteless. Girl, you are my angel.

A big thanks to Mahaveer Publishers, Binay Dutta and Dilip Jha without whose endeavour this book may not have been in your hands. Binay sir, you gave wings to my dreams.

Kiran, for reading out my drafts daily and encouraging me every moment. Shashank Tiwary from *Youth Diaries* for giving valuable feedback and he did that only because the male lead of the book coincidentally shares his name (don't kill me now).

Special thanks to Amit Sir and the entire team of *Isahitya* who gave me the opportunity to interview authors, my *Spectralhues* family for providing me the platform to write my heart out, Alok Vats Sir and I *News India* for giving me the chance to write on self-help topics.

My blogger family, especially Mr. Prasoon Verma, Neisha, Prasoon Khare for praising me for every crap I posted on my blogs.

Prakansh Rathaur, for such an amazing cover page.

My author friends, Jyotirmoy Mazumdar(author of 'Did She Love Me?'), Tanmay Kulshrestha (author of The Meth) and Ishita Bhown (author of 'Together') who helped me in every possible way. Thank you for being after me to pen down my words.

My English teachers at school, Ms. P. Andrews, Mrs. Dey and Ms. Richa Sinha for igniting in me the power of expressing my thoughts.

My friends who have been there with me at every step of my life, Upasana, Anu, Jain, Raaj, Shivika, Sandy, Mayank. To my gang of girlies at hostel, Monica, Khushboo, Nehul, Dolly, Priyanka for tolerating my mood swings while I wrote this book.

To my college, GLBITM, Greater Noida, especially the Department of Mechanical Engineering for helping me balance my studies and writing.

Apologies to all the people I have missed out on, believe me each one of you is an integral part of my life and your support has helped me achieve all this.

Prologue

The wind blew hard. I could see everybody running around for shelter. The leaves were flying in the air at high pace. I almost felt like plunging into the wind and taking in the anger of Nature into me. The rains would be coming soon, I thought. I stood still at the window side staring at the scene outside. I had nothing to do. The sandwiches prepared by Mum had already gone cold and the Fanta kept on the table had lost its fizz. I walked around the room and again came back to the place where I had been standing earlier.

My life had been going through just like the wind. There was a lot of chaos and hustle and bustle around. It was all messed up. I knew not what to do. I was helpless and had no destination to head to. I wish life could end now. Couldn't the Almighty consume the whole planet? We would all get finished up in one go. Damn! I was a coward to kill myself and I am so mean to get everyone killed just because there is no happiness in my life.

It started raining and the wind blew open the window with great thrust. I could feel the rain drops on my face now. It made me remember the time when love had first entered my life. Amazing, how love came and went away from my life on a rainy day. Rain had a big connection with me. It brought the best and worst moments in my life.

The clouds were crying their heart out. I wished I could do the same. Vishal had left me today. Does asking for true love seem a lot to God? Don't I deserve a man who would sweep me off my feet? Inside my heart was burning. Amazingly there were no tears in my eyes. Why should I cry for a person who didn't value my love? I guess my life will end like this, without the presence of that special someone. I think God wants me to stay alone forever or is he giving me some kind of experience? Does he want to say that I should wait for someone better? Will I ever receive love in return? Or am I God's special child for whom he has made a special someone?

OVER CUPS OF COFFEE

Stop callin', stop callin', I don't wanna think anymore

I left my head and my heart on the dance floor

Stop callin', stop callin', I don't wanna talk anymore

I left my head and my heart on the dance floor

This was my cell phone shouting on top of its voice. I woke up, huffing and puffing but I couldn't find it. O God where the hell was my cell? It was disturbing me like anything and when I couldn't find it, I took the pillow and stuck it closest to my ears and went off to sleep. Few minutes later, I could hear it again. Unwillingly I woke up, started looking for my cell and finally found it vibrating in between the clothes in the laundry bag. I looked angrily at it. It gleefully smiled saying, "Vishakha calling." I wish I could kill this bitch. I looked at my watch. I have the habit of wearing my watch twenty-four hours.

"Yeah baby, morning," I chanted the daily ritual of wishing my bitchy best friend and my sole companion in every situation.

"Morning, is it Ms. Priyanka Bajaj?"

"For me it is. And it's just five minutes past noon," I replied in a defensive tone.

"Washing away my last birth's sins by having a friend like you. Nobody can win you," she replied irritated.

"I have heard this umpteen times. You don't need to remind me. Anyway, come to the point. Where are we heading to?"

"The weather is super sexy. I feel like having coffee. Meet me at Barista, CSM. Okay darling?"

"Yeah babes. I'll be right there in an hour. See ya. Bye!"

"Bye. Muah."

Vishakha's call always ended like this. I hated her excessive cajoling and kissing. I knew she wasn't lesbian. She stared at boys and had a long list of boyfriends that their count passed the count of her shoe collection. She wasn't bisexual but then she had the habit of sending me kisses through messages daily even after knowing that I was averse to such acts of hers. She reasoned that till the time she doesn't find the right guy she preferred giving her precious kisses to me as I would understand the true meaning of a kiss. I thought her to be insane and nothing else.

Forty minutes later I was standing in the women's compartment of Metro. How love changes your life! I hadn't stepped into the ladies compartment since their existence till now as I was always accompanied by Vishal or most of the time he would drop me on his bike. In fact I was travelling in a Metro after a gap of around two months which is quite unusual for Delhites or people living close to Delhi like me. I have been putting up at Noida since the last four years. I reached Sector 18 Metro Station. I hate such places. This place is extremely crowded with couples hovering around in every possible place, especially on weekends. Students and office goers arrive here to freshen up whenever they get an off.

I saw Vishakha standing at the security check. She looked a true fashionista from top to bottom with the best shoes and the best dress on. I was sure she would sway away many boys today. And then I would have to handle all the guys who would follow us till home.

She almost squeaked when she saw me.

"Hi baby," she shouted in public and gave me a tight hug as if we were meeting after ages.

We sat on the corner table. I sat (read jumped) on the couch as I was tired of standing in the Metro. Vishakha gave me a 'Not again' look.

"So how has it been?" she asked me.

"My second boyfriend dumped me yesterday," I replied bluntly.

"What the hell is this? Don't give me this crap again, Priyanka."

"Well this is the truth. He said it isn't working any more. I think he has lost interest in me. I tried to reason out with him but he isn't ready for any discussion. I am seriously tired of this breakup thing. I don't want to be in love any more and I don't even know how to react at this moment. I am stunned by the turn of events."

"Girl, I am telling you he has found another bitch. Bloody bastard," Vishakha replied in her usual tone that I was accustomed to, but not the cafe people. Few of them turned around to see who was blabbering around so much.

"Please lower your voice Vish. We are in a public place," I said, almost pleading to her.

"Yeah, fine. I am going to have Mojito. What about you?"

"Whatever you wish to treat me with," I replied in a low tone.

"Your favourite, sadly boring, Cafe Mocha."

"Yeah. As you wish," I replied.

Stop callin, 'stop callin, 'I don't wanna think any more
I left my head and my heart on the dance floor
Stop callin, 'stop callin, 'I don't wanna talk any more
I left my head and my heart on the dance floor.

My phone rang again. I could see many a face turn around and a frown form on Vish's face. She hated this tone but I loved Lady Gaga.

"For heaven's sake keep some sophisticated tone. And please, whenever you are with me, keep your cell on vibration mode. I am fed up of Lady Gaga," Vishakha said in an irritated tone.

"Girl, she rocks. I love her carefree attitude," I said, taking Lady Gaga's side.

I picked up the call. It was some client asking about her wedding gown. And by the way did I tell you I am a B.Com. graduate from SRCC but got stuck in fabrics because I felt it brings out my creativity. I love designing clothes. And so with a small capital invested by my highly intellectual and influential C.A. Dad, I started on with my own workshop where I experiment with colours and fabrics. Vish enjoys the position of being my friend since she gets her dress designed free of cost most of the time. I have even enrolled for a one-year fashion designing course at NIFT and I am totally in love with my profession.

Dad always wanted me to be a C.A. just like him so that I could head the plush big office he owns but then all dreams aren't meant to come true. After three failed attempts at IPCC, I gave up on being a C.A. some day and thank God I did it because it made me search for my passion and I found it in fashion designing. I guess maybe one fine day my brother is going to realise his dream.

We walked out of Barista. Vish stopped by at Westside. She had to buy a new dress for her date tonight. Unfortunately I wasn't available for her this time as I had been busy with a lot of assignments and because of this I had heard all kind of abuses from her since the past week. She took an hour to select one dress; I would have chosen ten by now.

We walked out of CSM (Centre Stage Mall) only to find that it had been raining cats and dogs. Rain had to be after my life every time. I wanted no more of rain.

"Not again," I cried out.

"Shut up, silly woman. C'mon, let's go out and get wet. It's such a great weather outside."

"Yes of course, why not? You need to wash away your sins in the rain," I smirked.

"Whatever. Stuff this packet in your bag or my new tunic will get spoiled."

Before I could resist, she had already taken my hand and pushed me out in the rain. She hopped about like crazy. I took in the raindrops. They were soothing and refreshing. I could feel every drop touch my body. It was raining heavily and I was feeling a bit cold. I didn't even realise that I had tears in my eyes. They were draining out of my eyes like hell. I hadn't come out of my breakup till now. It was tough to be single again especially when the person has been all around you almost twenty-four hours of the day.

Before I could react, I saw Shashank pass by in his grey coloured Santro. It was him for sure. I still remember his car number. DL 04 Z 8888. But what was he doing in Noida? After our breakup, I had never seen him at Noida. He didn't like Noida; he loved staying at Delhi but since my family shifted to Noida by the time we began dating four years back, he had no option than to come down here on weekends.

I stood still in the rain. All I could remember was the first time we had met four years back. It had been raining even then.

FLASHBACK: FOUR YEARS BACK

PHASE-I

THE RAIN

Dad had decided to shift to Noida. I was never in favour of leaving our South Extension flat for a new home in Sector 15, Noida. But Dad felt I would be safe here as we had been receiving threatening calls from unknown people. He knew that it was some official rivalry but he wanted to keep us safe. He started anew here. He established a new office here and brought a big house. This house was bigger than the one we had at South Ex. We had better environment here. With the shifting taking place, I started on to our new place in my newly gifted car with the driver. I wanted to set my room my way, so I had especially come here for a purpose. While returning, I asked the driver to take the road to Sector 18 CCD as I was dead tired and in extreme need of coffee.

It had been raining that day and the road was blocked with vehicles and so much public around. I asked the driver to park somewhere, while I would take his leave there itself as there was a lot of chaos on the road. I was always an impatient creature and even then, I couldn't wait for the car to get parked properly.

I ran about to look for CCD as I had been there almost one year back but by God's grace, I have a horrible road sense, so I couldn't exactly figure it out. I was walking in the middle of the road as if the road belonged to my Dad. Suddenly a trio of boys came in front of me and one of them bumped into me. Not only that, he even dropped the Cola drink he was carrying with himself.

"Hey, can't you see and walk? You've spoiled my shirt," I shouted at him. The pitch of my voice was so high that many people stopped by to look at the scene I had created.

"I am really sorry Ma'am. I didn't do that intentionally," the boy spoke.

"Look, I am really not interested in knowing if you have done this intentionally or not. You should at least look and walk. Now how am I going to stay like this for more than an hour? Idiot guy," I said in an irritated tone.

"I know you must be annoyed with what happened to you but please accept my apologies; they are seriously genuine."

I snatched the can from his hand and threw the remaining Cola on his T-shirt. He looked at me with wide open eyes. He was more than shocked; I could tell this from his eyes. I guess he didn't expect such behaviour from me.

"Serves you right," I crashed the can with my sneakers while I spoke to him.

I walked my way. He walked his way.

I sat in the corner seat of CCD, mourning over the fact that my favourite white shirt had been ruined. No way would it look the way it used to earlier. I sipped in the cold coffee, messaging Vish about the whole incident. She was happy that I had taken my revenge on that guy.

And then out of nowhere, the boy with whom I had fought thirty minutes ago, entered CCD. Why was he coming towards me? Would he insult me in CCD? I was scared but didn't let it show on my face.

"Hi! Shashank here and you?" he addressed me.

I gulped in some more coffee and finally uttered, "Priyanka."

"Well I stopped by to offer you this," he handed over a packet to me. I opened it to find that there was a navy blue top. I was surprised and felt all the more guilty about my behaviour.

"Thanks a ton for this, but really there wasn't a need for this. And I am really sorry for what I did to you outside," I spoke in one breath. I could see the spot on his grey T-shirt.

"No, that's okay. Anyone would do the same. It was my mistake after all and in rainy season, avoid wearing white. It gets dirty easily," he said, smiling at me.

"So that is why you gave me a dark shade so that next time you could throw Cola at me again?" I asked questioningly.

And we began to laugh.

We went to GIP, another mall in Sector 18, where I changed and he asked me to join him for coffee. I was already bowled over by him and his polished manners. And I agreed instantly to his offer, which girl would deny? He was good looking, I noticed.

We sat at CCD again.

"So, care to give an intro about yourself?"

"I am Priyanka Bajaj studying in Std. XII, Commerce stream from Amity International School, Saket," I said.

"Shashank Agrawal, student of XII, Science stream, Apeejay School, Saket."

"Great. We come to the same area every morning. So Science, eh? Medical or engineering?"

"Engineering," he answered in one shot.

"Cool, great plans," I replied.

"What about you? Charted Accountant or CS or something else?" he asked.

"I'll be just like my Dad. I have always wanted to be a C.A. After all, who is going to shoulder his responsibilities after he gets old?"

"Wow! I like that thought. My Dad is a big businessman but I have no interest in his business. I want to crack IIT. Engineering is my passion. And if you don't mind, we can meet some time after school."

I blushed when he said this. Maybe he liked me just the way I had been daydreaming about him.

He shook me to wake me up from my dreams.

"I am sorry if I annoyed you," he said apologetically.

"No, no. I am completely fine and it would be a pleasure to catch up with you," I replied. Only a fool could say no to him.

"So apart from the general info, what else do you like?" he asked with the curvy smile on his face that made me forget myself.

"Anything and everything that makes me happy," I said cheerfully.

"You seem to be quite in love with life."

"Of course, I love myself and enjoy life to the fullest," I said what I felt.

We chatted for thirty minutes more and in between this I felt as if he was the man I had been searching for. I had fallen for him. I kept noticing his way of speaking, his lip movement and the killer smile that he had. I didn't want to leave but it was getting late. The rain had stopped by then. He walked to drop me till the parking area. I wished if he would ask for my cell number but he didn't and I was feeling too shy to even ask for his. He opened the car door for me and we waved to each other. This wasn't the final goodbye; my heart knew we would meet again.

He walked his way and I went my way.

I came back home dreamy eyed. My Mom noticed it. I was behaving oddly during dinner time. I couldn't even serve myself properly. I dropped the curry twice. Normally I finish food early but that day I couldn't even finish one *chapatti* easily. I tried to sleep but couldn't. I kept on tossing and turning all night. It was one of the most beautiful nights of my life. I went on rewinding the whole incident in my mind. His gestures, expressions, his eyes that spoke a lot; he was the man I would be complete with. Sleep came late that night.

"Hey beautiful, you are the only girl I've ever wanted. You are the person who made me realise that love is such a great emotion. Love binds this world; it unites two souls and somehow my soul has gone to you. I don't have beautiful words to say today as your beauty outpasses everything present in this world. I may not be the perfect guy for you but I want to make every day perfect for you. I love you, Priyanka. And I wouldn't want to wait for anything today. All I can ask you is, will you marry me?"

"Yes Shashank," that was all I could say but why was I hearing so much of loud music. Why had the low, soft, romantic music turned to hiphop suddenly?

Slap! Slap! Did I just feel a slap on my face?

I opened my eyes, touched my cheeks and looked around. Damn, it was just a dream! My brother was staring at me.

"Bebot bebot bet

Bebot bebot bet

Bebot bebot bet!"

I could hear the Black Eyed Peas in the background. It was my alarm tone and since I hadn't switched it off, my brother had got irritated and slapped me hard.

"Why are you staring at me?" I asked my brother.

"Because you were muttering something while sleeping and you hadn't switched off the alarm. I hate it when you do this," he said in an infuriated tone.

"So what was the need to slap me hard? I am your elder sis, okay?" I replied in anger.

"Silly elder sis who mutters stupid words in sleep. And by the way; who is Shashank? I've never heard of any friend by this name," he asked questioningly. Even in his sleep he didn't forget to investigate on me. I am telling you all the brothers of India should be sent to CID. There will be less of crime against women.

"Even I don't know, I was in the middle of a dream," I lied to my bro. Did I just lie to my bro for a guy whom I met yesterday? Man, he was making me go crazy.

In school I narrated the whole incident to Vish. She was surprised to know that a boy had done so much to me. I didn't hear what Sir said in the Accounts class. In the book I saw his face, the last day's event were passing through my mind back and forth. I could hardly concentrate in any of the classes the whole day.

"Priyanka, are you present in the class?" my English teacher aroused me once.

"Yes Ma'am," I replied, awakening from my thoughts.

"Then could you please explain to the class the message that '*The Enemy*' gives?"

"Umm...Ma'am it gives us the... umm..the message of humanity," I spoke up with a lot of difficulty.

"And?" Ma'am looked into my eyes and I was ashamed of not being able to answer for the first time in her class.

"Next time please pay a little more attention in my class. I don't expect this from students like you."

"Sorry Ma'am."

I sat down and she went on with teaching us and telling us all about the chapter. I had become so lost in my thoughts that I wasn't able to concentrate on anything. I was such a big fool to fall for a guy whom I didn't even know for more than a day; someone whose contact information was unknown to me. I was crazy. Maybe this was the aura of first love as everyone says. All logics had fallen off my mind since I had met Shashank.

❖ ❖ ❖

Five days passed by and I didn't hear any news about Shashank. I was in a confused state— whether I should drop thinking about him or I should continue in the hope that he would meet me some day? I couldn't take all this any more. I called up Vish.

"Hey!"

"What's up babe?" Vishakha replied.

"Nothing much. Could you please come home? I am feeling a bit lonely."

"Aww..my baby. What happened? I'll be there in a jiffy, just don't worry."

"Hmm.. Just a little off colour. I'll tell you when you come. Bye. I'll be waiting for you," I said as I hung up.

Fifteen minutes later, I was crying like a kid with Vish holding my hand and trying to cheer me up.

"Don't cry sweetheart, we will find him for you. What's his full name?"

"Shashank Agrawal."

"Cool! Apeejay, Saket isn't out of reach. I'll bring every information about him. And promise me you will move on if you get to know that he is committed, okay?"

"That's not easy, Vish," I sniffed. "But I'll try."

"Okay, now cheer up, darling. Try to connect with him through Orkut. He must be present in their school community."

Man, why hadn't I thought of Orkut till now? I had seriously lost my brains. Just the way people are crazy about Facebook, few years back it was Orkut that ruled the social networking arena.

I took my laptop and logged into Orkut. We searched for the Apeejay School, Saket Community and yes I found my prince. Shashank Agrawal. Relationship Status: Single. Thank God, I smiled at Vish. And then I started jumping on the bed. Yes! Yes! Yes! I was elated to see him. We tried to open his pics but they were locked.

"Send him a request," Vish ordered me.

"Noooooo!"

"But why?"

"I'll sound too desperate," I spoke, making faces.

"You are desperate, Priyanka. Do what you wish and don't come to me, crying for your Prince Charming next time. I am going, bye."

Vish banged the door hard and I went back to admiring my prince.

Shashank Agrawal

Lifezz a long race...

Scraps: 1232

Relationship Status:Single

(I was happy to read this. Yay!)

Birthday: 2nd April (17years old)

(So he was an Arian. Cool. I was around 1.5 months younger to him)

His Social Profile said:

Smoking: No

Drinking: No

(I heaved a sigh of relief. Thank God he didn't drink or smoke)

Pets: I love my pets

(Me too)

Passions: Cracking Maths problems, listening to music, basketball, hitting the gym, driving my car.

(Yuck! Who loves solving Maths problems but hey, he loves music just like me. One day I would love to see him play basketball or may be learn from him)

Books: *Wings of Fire* by Dr. APJ Abdul Kalam.

(I liked reading books but I hadn't read this. I will ask him to give me his copy)

Music: Bryan Adams, Atif and anything that is soothing to ears.

(Wow! We were so similar; even I loved Bryan Adams)

Cuisines: Mom-made food, Punjabi and Rajasthani food, a little bit of Chinese.

(I'll make him love Chinese and Italian, I thought)

Movies: *A Walk To Remember, Jab We Met.*

(I loved these movies too. Yay! Another similarity)

TV Shows: Roadies.

Personal Profile:

Eye Colour: Black

Hair Colour: Black

Best feature: Eyes

(I stared at his Display Pic, especially his eyes. Yes, they were truly the best feature in him)

Turn ons: Candlelight Dinner, Intelligence Dancing, Long Hair.

(Long Hair...I checked my hair in the mirror. It was little more than shoulder length. I pledged to take care of my hair, so that they could become long soon)

Turn Offs: Display of affection, wealth.

(Wealth? Why did it turn him off? His Dad was a wealthy businessman, then why such kind of an indication? May be he didn't like showing off one's wealth. He's so down to earth)

I slept thinking about him all the more. And I didn't forget to oil my hair, so that they would start looking better.

"Bebot bebot bet

Bebot bebot bet

Bebot bebot bet!"

The alarm rang. I woke up and the first thing that I did was change the alarm tone. I changed it to Bryan Adam's 'Summer of 69'. It was a Saturday, so I had an off from school. I applied hair mask and face pack for the first time in my life. Till that time the only cosmetic I used was a lip balm even it doesn't come under the makeup category. I had taken Vish's suggestion to use the best of beauty products. That day I spent two hours to groom myself.

I called up Vish.

"Hey babes, what's up?" Vish asked in her normal cheerful tone.

"I want you to accompany me to a good saloon."

"Whaaaaaaaaaaat? Pardon me please, did I hear the right thing?" Vish replied. She was stunned to hear all this from me.

"Yes. Come on stop reacting like this and get ready. I am reaching your home in fifteen minutes."

"Yo! I am surprised to know that a boy can bring so many changes in you. I am already dressed well. Come soon."

That day I got my eyebrows made and my upper lips too. Man it hurt awfully. I got myself waxed. Facial, hair spa and a new hairstyle followed soon. I looked better and it felt good to look good.

I was all smiles at seeing myself and Vish hugged me. "I love you. And I have faith in your love for Shashank. Till now I thought you were simply infatuated with him but today my instincts make me feel that you do love him. You'll get him one day for sure," she said lovingly to me.

Her words made me feel better. I was glad to have a friend like her.

We roamed around in Select City Walk and clicked many pics. I wanted to keep these memories. After all, I would be leaving this place for my new home in Noida. I wouldn't be able to meet Vish every day in the evening from now on. It would be just plain evenings with Bhai and Buster. Buster is my super cute dog.

I came back with added confidence. I logged into my Orkut account to upload today's pics and have a look at my Prince Charming again. One friend request. OMG! It was from Shashank. My hands went cold and I couldn't even move the cursor to accept his request. I kept staring at him. Was this a dream? I pinched myself. Ouch! That hurt. Yes, it was true. Yes! Yes! I jumped on my bed. Switched on to some random music and started dancing away. I stopped to accept his request and danced some more. I changed my DP and uploaded the latest pics. Now I had full access to his photos. I opened his albums; one by one I saw them all. He was the school captain I came to know. I was impressed even more.

"You look great and I can see my daughter is super happy today", Mom said while talking to me at dinner.

I blushed and said, "Thanks Mom."

"Did I just see my daughter getting pink?" she teased me.

"No Mom, but I am feeling too good."

"Aww..I am so happy for you, sweetheart," Mom said hugging me lovingly.

I logged in to my account before sleeping. Somebody had scrapped me. My number of scraps had increased by one. I clicked on my Scrapbook. I wished it would be from Shashank.

Hey...It's great catching up with you on Orkut. I almost thought that I would not be able to talk to you henceforth, but thanks to Orkut, I've got my lost friend back. How have you been? I would love to meet you some time online. Do let me know the timing.

P.S: You look great in your new DP

Yes, it was from him. And he had not only showed interest in meeting me, but he had complimented me on my looks too. This was a déjà vu moment for me. I was on cloud nine. It had been sent nineteen minutes ago. I despised myself for logging in twenty minutes late. I wished him to be online. I gathered courage to reply to his scrap.

Hi...I am doing well. What about you? How is school going? And I'm glad we met here. I'll be online tomorrow evening at 5 p.m and night at 10 p.m. We are shifting tomorrow to Noida.

P.S: Thanks for the compliment

I clicked on the Send tab. I waited for thirty minutes for his reply, refreshed my Scrapbook umpteen times. But I guess he had gone. As I went to bed that night, I felt happy about being able to contact him and a little dejected at not being able to chat with him. But I had the assurance that we would chat soon. I slept peacefully that day.

It took long to do the shifting the next day. It had been very hectic. I dropped on to a couch and slept when I knew not. I slept for, I don't know how long but when I woke up, the first thing I did was to look at my watch. It said 9 p.m. Man, I had missed my online date with Shashank. Yes, that is what I felt like calling it. I hurried up with dinner and logged on to Orkut. My number of scraps had increased by ten. I saw a few scraps from him.

The first one said: Hey, there?

The second one said: I am sorry I came late. I think you've gone.

The third one said: I'll come at ten. Hope to see you around at that time. I hope the shifting went on well. And I am hale and hearty as always. I am wearing the grey T-shirt today and it still has the Cola mark.

P.S: You are welcome, young lady. It is a pleasure to compliment you. You are seriously looking good, better than last Sunday.

I didn't want to lose my second chance and I waited for him to arrive. My cell showed 10:07 p.m. I refreshed my Orkut home page.

"Hi! there?"

This was the scrap I had been waiting for. He had come online especially for me. "Hi! I am so glad to have you here. I am sorry I couldn't make it in the evening."

"That's okay. I can understand, you must have been busy with shifting."

"Hmm... so how has the week been?" I asked.

"Lots of assignments at coaching, pressure at school, the workload is making me go crazy," he replied.

"Ohh… sad. But you'll do. You are hardworking and you have the passion to do it," I said reassuring him.

"Maybe you are right. Chuck out studies. Tell me, how does staying at Noida feel?"

"Well, in the first place I never wanted to be here. School would be extremely far now. Dad wants me to shift to the Amity, Noida but I don't want to. And I love Delhi. I have been there since childhood," I gave him an obvious response. Shifting from a place that has been your home for years definitely makes you depressing. My home in South Ex. had been a spectator to so many memories. That was the only place I could refer to as my home. Nevertheless I had to be here, as the saying goes 'Home is where Mom is.' Change is the law of Nature and as humans, we are bound to accept them, but it's not easy as it sounds. Adjusting to a whole new environment is difficult.

"Yeah… I can understand but you can't do anything. You'll begin to like it soon. And Delhi isn't far; you can come around anytime. Personally speaking, even I don't like Noida."

"Really? But then what were you doing here last Sunday?" I asked questioningly.

"I had come to my aunt's place. She lives in Noida. When I met you, I was with my cousins."

"Okay. So?"

I didn't know what to say next.

"So, did you miss me?"

What? Had I read it right? Was he asking me if I missed him or not? Yes, I missed you like hell. This is what I wanted to say but I ended up saying, "What? I am sorry I didn't get you."

"Nothing. Just kidding. Can I ask you a question?"

I hope he wasn't going to ask something that I wouldn't be able to answer. "Sure. What do you want to ask?"

"When I logged into my account yesterday, I found you in my recent visitors. If you had found me on Orkut, why hadn't you send me request? Is it related to girl ego or something else?"

How could I tell him that it would have meant showing me as another desperate girl. Man, girls don't send request.

"Hehehe... Don't you know girls don't send request? And I was in a confusion whether you would recognise me or not."

"Is that so? I can never forget the first girl who tried to malign my image in public," he replied.

"OMG! Is that so?" I asked.

"Yes."

"I am really sorry for it *wink*."

"That's okay. I easily forgive people.*wink*"

I don't know for how long we talked. It looked as if the clock had stopped. The feeling was wonderful. Reading his scraps, I felt as if we were talking face to face. Twice, my brother woke up, looked at me and saw me working on the laptop.

"Are you not going to sleep tonight?" he asked sleepily.

"Yes, I will. You know I had slept earlier, so I am not getting sleep," I said irritated as he was interfering in the beautiful moments I was experiencing. He got back to sleeping and I went back to staring at my laptop's screen. We talked for long that night. I didn't want the conversation to stop, but we had to end it. We bade each other goodbye with a promise to meet again. I read out his scarps for 'n' number of times. At that time I wished if Orkut had the privacy lock in which only I could view my scrapbook. I didn't want anyone else to see our conversation. Finally I closed my laptop, plugged in my headphones and went off to sleep listening to slow and romantic songs. It took me an hour to get down to sleep that day as all I did was think about him.

I had to wake up early the next morning as reaching South Delhi from Noida takes time. It was a typical task but Shashank's thoughts made me do everything. I was extremely content and happy with my life. And finally I could pay attention to my subjects as in my heart of hearts, I knew that we were meant to be together.

That day when I was returning from school, lost in my (or rather his) thoughts, I found a boy standing outside the school gate. Was I dreaming or was it really Shashank? He looked great in uniform too. There are some people who always look good, whatever they wear. It just suits them. I guess they know the art of carrying themselves; Shashank was one of them. I still couldn't believe my eyes that Shashank was standing. I almost thought that I was day dreaming and therefore walked past him. Maybe he hadn't expected such a reaction from me because he came running to me, calling my name, "Hey Priyanka, what's up with you. Didn't you? see me standing at the gate? And from what I could see, you were looking in my direction."

Finally I got my senses confirmed that he was really Shashank.

"Hi! I am sorry I didn't see you," I said smiling at him. Oh! God, why do I have to make a fool of myself when it is most uncalled for?

"So?"

"So?" I asked questioningly, not knowing what to say.

"I was going back home, so I just thought of catching up with you."

"Cool!" That is all I could say. Within me, my heart was jumping around but I couldn't even gather proper courage to talk to him.

"Mind walking back home together?" he asked.

"No, not at all. But perhaps you are forgetting the fact that I have shifted to Noida."

"I remember. I am going to my aunt's place so we can go together. Now is it okay?"

"Yes but what about your coaching?" I asked, perplexed. I didn't want him to ignore his studies because of me.

"Don't worry about that. I'll manage sweetie," he smiled.

I nodded in approval and went with him. I told my brother and driver to leave and gave the excuse of having some extra work. It felt awesome to know that he was skipping his coaching to drop me to Noida.

He opened his car door for me but I refused. "What happened?" his eyes questioned.

I pointed at the bus and told him, "Let's catch the bus."

He smiled, closed the car door and threw the car keys at his friend. His friend winked at him and saluted me. He took my hand, I blushed and smiled shyly. We walked and I could hear lots of hooting in the background but I didn't bother about it. All I knew was that I was with the man of my life and that was all that mattered to me.

We entered the bus. Unfortunately we didn't get a seat. The bus was jam-packed. He stood behind me and then came a boy who must have been in his twenties and looked like a true roadside flirt. He stood just in front of me. As expected, he began the ritual of staring at me. I had by now become used to the unruly behaviour of boys in Delhi and I thought I would be able to tackle him as always. I had often applied this technique and it had worked for me. The moment a guy begins to stare at you, stare him back. I tried this out with him too but he didn't stop his misdeeds. But by this time my Prince Charming had already realised what was going on and like a true gentleman, he left his place and stood right in front of me. Such acts by him always made me blush and this moment was no exception. I loved the fact that he was protective about me.

We stopped at McDonalds. The happiness within me had already filled my stomach. I ate half the burger and left the remaining.

"What happened? You don't feel like eating anymore?"

"No, I am stuffed," I replied dramatically, placing my hands around my neck.

And that very moment he picked my half-eaten burger and took a bite from it.

"Do you still want to leave it unfinished?" He asked me with a knowing and a very familiar smile.

I smiled shyly, took the burger and began eating it from the point he had left. His cell rang and he went out to take the call. I noticed his ringtone was the whistling tune of *Kuch Kuch Hota Hai*. Meanwhile I took a sip from his cold coffee. I don't know why, but it tasted yummier than mine.

We took another bus. Thankfully, this time we got two seats. He passed on an earphone to me and plugged in the other one in his ear. The song that played was '*Ae mere humsafar*' from *Qayamat Se Qayamat Tak*. I was quite surprised to find him hearing to these songs.

"Do you listen to the 90s songs?"

"Yes I love old songs, 70s, 80s, and 90s. That era had a different kind of romance, isn't it? It used to be eternal."

I kept on looking at him and I didn't even realise when I fell asleep on his shoulder. Amazingly I had my first date in school uniform but it was beautiful. He woke me up, touching my cheeks and telling me that our destination had come. We climbed down the bus.

"Why did you refuse to come in my car?"

"Just like that, no particular reason," I said.

"Don't worry. You'll never have to fret about your safety till I am present and I would do to no harm to you even in my dreams. But I understand you're a girl and you must be scared as there have been lots of cases of such kind and I respect your feelings. I'll never let you down, trust me."

I looked into his eyes, and saw they spoke a lot. I was overwhelmed with emotions. And that day onwards, I started respecting him. I respected him for what he was and what he did for me. I had finally found the man I could look up to after my Dad. He had taken a portion of my thoughts. He resided in my heart and mind 24 × 7.

"Thanks," that was all I could say, even though I wanted to speak a lot. Our eyes conversed while we lost on words. I turned back to move towards the entrance of my home. I looked at him and waved. He reciprocated the same. I kept on looking till he vanished from my lane and my sight.

I entered my house and took a refreshing bath. I found myself smiling for no reason and I couldn't even look at myself in the mirror. Something was making me blush and the reason was Shashank.

I logged in to my Orkut account to take a look at him before going to sleep. He had left me a scrap : *Hey, it was really great to have your company today evening. I'll wait for some more rides with you.*

*Hope you would also like to accompany me sometime again. And I hope even you had a good time with me (I know I am a good listener and a good entertainer as well*laughing*). Take rest, you must have been tired.*

Catch ya later.

Bye, take care.

Surprisingly, we still interacted with each other through Orkut. We didn't have each other's cell number. Neither did I ask, nor did he. We were behaving rather oddly considering the fact that we were 21st century teens but we all know that love is not restricted by time and circumstances.

The next day as I entered school, I could hear a lot of hooting going on. My girly group surrounded me. "So you and Shashank are a couple now?"

"How was the date yesterday?"

"Cunning woman, you didn't tell us about it."

"Hey give us a treat."

Questions like these kept on popping up and I could hear the song, '*Chup chup reh ke tune rakkha apna mouth shut*' from the movie MP3 (Mera Pehla Pehla Pyaar) in the background. I couldn't handle this any more and shouted on the top of my voice. Everybody stopped and stared at me. "There is nothing between Shashank and me. Got it?" I stamped my feet and went into my class.

I didn't want anybody to know about us. I just didn't want this. I don't know why but I just wanted to keep Shashank to myself only. This was my personal life and I didn't want anyone to comment on our relationship because I knew everyone would consider it as just another fling. They would never understand that our love was eternal. He would be my first and last love.

THE RAIN HANGOVER

"Priyanka, let's go now. You are shivering," Vish shook me hard and I came back to my senses.

We ran towards the Metro station. I was kind of numb. The rain had made me cold. I was trembling like hell. My mind was racing between Shashank and Vishal. I wanted peace; a state of tranquillity is what I wished for.

"Are you alright?" Vish had sensed there was something wrong.

"I saw Shashank's car outside CSM," I blurted out.

"He must have come back home. It's their semester break going on."

"Vish, the point is he hates this place. Even his aunt has shifted to Chandigarh now. What made him suddenly come here?" I asked. There were a horde of questions in my mind. Somehow it never ends with your ex. A mere mention or sight of him brings the old memories back that urge you to know about his present. The same feeling erupted in me. I had an impulsive desire to know what he was up to. What had brought him here?

"I don't know. Call him and check it out," she replied casually.

"Don't talk rubbish, Vish. We haven't talked since the past one year."

"That hasn't diminished your love for him in any way. Calling does no harm," she went on nonchalantly. Didn't she even guess that butterflies had begun to flutter in my stomach? I always went into a panic and anxious mode whenever the topic of Shashank came up. Shashank and this state of mine were interconnected. It didn't happen with anyone else, except Shashank.

"But Vish, we broke up two years back," I said in an uneasy tone.

"Yes but you are still stuck up on him. You haven't moved on, have you?" she said as she finally sat up to do some serious talking. That is how she is; she won't listen to me properly in the first half of the story, remaining indifferent to what I keep jabbering about. She keeps on playing Angry Birds, munching away a bowlful of potato wafers. And then suddenly, she remembers that her best friend is actually in trouble, so she sits down straight, crossing her legs and tying her hair in a bun. After acquiring this position only, she will be prepared to give some vital suggestions on a problem. And she doesn't care about the location. She will sit like this anywhere, whether it is home or a high-end restaurant or a coffee house. Today it was the Metro station.

"I am supposed to have moved on. I did try to and I was towards the achievement but Vishal's decision makes me feel the other way," I said in a drained out voice.

"You still haven't told me how things ran into rough weather between Vishal and you."

"Vish, it's a long story and it will take time."

"I have all the time to listen to you."

We headed towards my home. I changed as I was totally drenched in rain. Mom had just made muffins for us and I loved the warm muffins that she prepared.

"So begin your story now. I want to know everything."

"There was something wrong since the last three months Vish, but like always, I sensed it one month back. He played cunningly. We weren't even communicating properly, and finally, he broke up yesterday after I came to know about his girlfriend."

"What? Did you say his girlfriend? Then what were you? Was he trying to double cross you?"

I could see a mixture of horror and anger in her expressions. "Yes, somewhat like that."

Before I could speak more, her cell rang. She had to go home and my story was left midway.

After she had left, all I did was to think. I thought about Vishal and the times we had spent. And then it struck me that I had never accepted him as my love. I had tried but I had never taken him as my man. I liked his friendship, his talks but that was all. I remembered Vish's words, "You could never forget Shashank anyway. Calling does no harm."

Her words kept on haunting me all night and I went back to the time when we had become a couple officially, the time we had spent together, moments with him and without him. I turned on the rewind button in my mind.

FLASHBACK: FOUR YEARS BACK

PHASE-II

LIFE, LOVE AND MUSIC

Shashank and I became inseparable. There was an unknown vibe that bonded us together. We had endless conversations on Orkut, Yahoo and Gtalk. Day and night, Shashank would be on my mind, but somehow I felt that we should get connected through phone. As of now, we could talk only when we came online but it often happened that one of us wasn't able to make it on time. Having each other's cell number would have helped in better contact. I guess we were a shy couple who took ages to take a small step. Maybe Shashank was always caught in his gentlemanly etiquettes. Nevertheless, he had taken the step finally.

One day, the moment I had been waiting for since long, occurred. We were chatting away normally on Orkut when he suddenly asked for my cell number. I wanted to pass it on but didn't know how to react to his scrap. I always behaved abnormally when I needed to put up a proper show. I abruptly logged out after reading his scrap that said he wanted to have telephonic conversations with me. But a day after, in one of those lost-in-his thoughts evening, I messaged him my number on Orkut. I waited restlessly for his call. In one of our conversations he had mentioned that he used Hutch (years back Vodafone was called Hutch. Oh and did you know Hutch had another name too and that was Essar when it first came into the market? Man, my general knowledge as well as memory is too good, collars up) and after that I always looked for some unknown number calling me, especially Hutch. I checked my phone umpteen times. I didn't leave my phone lying anywhere because should Mom or my bro had picked it up by mistake, I would have been murdered.

And finally the most awaited call of my life arrived. I was studying (read sleeping) in my Accounts coaching when my cell vibrated twice but I didn't seem to notice it. Of course I wouldn't have, I was in a deep slumber. But I did have a habit of checking my cell phone after my coaching ended, reason being my cell would be flooded with new messages in a matter of two hours and I seriously had to keep my message tone on silent. So what I am trying to say is that when I checked my call list, I saw two missed calls. And I didn't think that it could be from Shashank, I thought it must be some ghost call from Vish. Before giving it a second thought I moved out of my class and then my cell vibrated again. Fortunately, I caught it and picked up, "Hullo"

"Priyanka?"

I heard a boy's voice and like always I thought it was some random guy trying his luck.

"Who do you want to talk to?" I questioned boldly. Silly me, couldn't even recognize his voice.

"Priyanka, this is Shashank... Shashank Agrawal. Ring a bell!"

Oh yes, the moment had finally arrived and it came in the most sudden way. I could hardly speak but with a little difficulty I spoke, "Yes of course. Hi! Shashank. How are you?"

"All well. Are you out?"

"Yes I am in my coaching centre. And I am sorry I couldn't pick up your call as I was in the middle of a lecture," I replied. How could I tell him that I hadn't even sensed one bit of vibration?

"That's okay. Even my coaching begins in a few minutes."

"Oh! I should hang up then," I said dejectedly. I wanted to talk to him.

"Hmm...You should also get going. If you are free, may I call you after an hour?"

"Yeah... sure," I replied, my mood upbeat after being from down in the dumps.

"Bye Priyanka."

"Bye!"

That night we talked for an hour and learnt a lot about each other. Cupid had struck both of us. Both of us knew what we felt for each other. There are a few relations that need no definition, Shashank and mine was something similar to it.

At last, my prayers were answered. The D-day arrived when I received the official proposal from Shashank for marriage. It would sound awkward but that was how it was. We weren't just boyfriend-girlfriend who see each other for some time and part ways. We considered our love timeless. I accept we were just seventeen but we were 'the one and only soul mate' types.

I was returning from my coaching. My class had been abruptly cancelled as sir had met with an accident on the way to coaching class. I felt sorry for him but then it felt good to have got a day off. Plus this also helped me escape the tension of not attempting the Accounts questions. I hopped on the stairs and instantly sent a message to Shashank, telling him about the good luck that had come my way. In a minute, I received a call from him.

"Hey!" I spoke gleefully.

"Hi! Priya!"

"Don't call me Priya. You may call me Pia," I said getting annoyed. I just hated to be addressed by this name.

"And why so? What's wrong with Priya?" he questioned.

"I just don't like it. It's sounds as if I am a thirty-year old aunty," I said in a displeased manner.

"Okay Ms. Priyanka Bajaj," he said, singing away my name.

I giggled.

"Why are you laughing? Do I sound funny?"

"No, no. I wasn't laughing at you. I just liked the way you called my name," I said as I giggled again.

"Oh, is it? I am honoured Mrs. Priyanka Agrawal."

"What? What did you just say?" I uttered. I was shocked. In fact my senses seemed to have stopped working. This was the moment I had been waiting for, but it had come so suddenly that it had left me numb. Yes, my happiness was beyond limits that day.

"Ah! Don't you like this name, Mrs. Priyanka Shashank Agrawal? This name sounds better," he said as he chuckled. He wasn't nervous while he said this. Most of the boys get tense while proposing to a girl but Shashank's voice showed full confidence. I guess that was because he knew I would not deny. Both of us knew about our feelings for each other and the only thing that remained was expressing it through words.

"No, it doesn't," I said mischievously.

"Really? May be then, I should change Nitika's name," he said cunningly.

"No, you idiot. Why are you spoiling her life?"

"You aren't ready. So I'll have to find an alternative," he said as he played with me.

"There is absolutely no need for that, Mr. Shashank Bajaj."

"Why are you changing my name?"

"Because it's unfair to change a girl's name. On a different note, let's change your name," I said grinning hard.

"Then will you marry me?"

I could almost feel the intense love in his words and it felt as if we would get married that year itself.

"Yes."

I wonder why I fall short of words when I am overwhelmed with emotions.

"Priyanka, I love you."

"And you took so much time to say this," I said.

"Yes, because I wanted to make sure whether it was love or infatuation."

"So are you sure now?" I asked.

"Yes, I'm absolutely sure."

"And so am I," I replied. I wanted to hug him that very moment.

"So when is the date?" Shashank asked too eagerly.

"Whenever you say."

"In thirty minutes. Get ready."

"What? Are you crazy? You can't reach Noida in thirty minutes. It'll take you at least two hours at such a busy hour and I'm not bunking," I said going crazy.

"You don't worry about that. Just inform your Mom that you'll be getting late as class has been extended."

"But Shashank, it's risky. You don't need to drive fast. We can meet later. It's not that urgent," I said, getting worried about him.

"For me, it is. And please stop getting tensed about me. I will be fine. Just get ready," he said authoritatively.

"Okay, I will and please take care of yourself. Don't drive rash," I said as I hung up the call.

I looked at myself. I gave the impression of a wimp in my white capri and yellow top. No way could I go for a date in such an attire. I had a panic attack and I called up Vish, my saviour in every situation. "Vish, I am in urgent need of help. Shashank just proposed me and I said yes," I said in a monotone.

"Wow! Oh my God, that's so exciting. I am so happy for you, babes. Congratulations."

"Vish, that's alright. We can celebrate later on. The point is Shashank will be arriving here in thirty minutes and I'm not in my best attire. I just have 800 bucks in my wallet that can't buy me any good stuff. Help me out."

"Relax girl. Go for street shopping."

"What?" I asked with uncertainty.

"See, you really don't have any other option. Rather than freaking out, buy some stuff from Atta Market there. It's somewhat similar to Sarojini Nagar and should get you some good deal."

"Will that work out? Are you sure? And getting the right piece at once is something impossible for me, without your help," I said, going panicky again.

"I'm always there with you. Just go for the one that you think would make you look better. And you always have the right to be late. You are a girl," she replied, trying to motivate me.

"Thanks babe. You are always my saviour."

"Any time, gal. And I need a treat tomorrow."

"For sure. Bye!" I said as I hung up the call.

"Bye!"

Apart from the monsoon season, the month that I totally adore is November. A light whisk of cold wind is not only soothing, but also rejuvenating. It was early November and I was about to have a tryst with the man who had just proposed me for marriage. I was all done with getting ready almost before time. I had bought myself a good top and I looked fine. For the first time in my life I had ditched my sporty look all together. There was not a streak that could indicate that I was a total freak. I had never looked so girlie ever in my life, but then I was entirely different and I was in love with my new attire. Something within me made me feel the greatness of being a girl, the uniqueness that only an Indian girl can feel.

I sat at the coffee shop where we had met first and thought about the future when I would be having my daily morning coffee with him. What a bliss those moments would be!

Forty-five minutes had gone by since Shashank had called and I was getting too restless. So I thought of giving him a call though I was pretty sure that he must have got stuck in some jam. Nevertheless I could always ask if he would be taking some more time.

"Hello," an unknown male voice greeted me. I was taken by surprise.

"Shashank?"

"I am sorry Ma'am but the person you've called has met with an accident. We were trying to figure out his near ones until your call came. If possible, could you please come to Vinayak Hospital?"

"Yes, I am coming in a jiffy."

I ran across the road for an auto. Ugly thoughts kept on erupting in my mind. I had told him not to drive but who listens to me? God, why did this happen to him? Tears ran through my eyes as I waited for the driver to take me to the hospital. I reached there, huffing and puffing.

"Shashank Agrawal. In which room has he been shifted to?"

"I'm sorry ma'am but there's no such patient here."

How could that be? I had just received a call about him being there. As soon as I picked up my cell to call Shashank's number, I heard a voice calling out my name and I knew it was Shashank.

I turned around to saw him standing hale and hearty.

"You dog," I screamed at him. He began to laugh and I ran towards him and gave him a punch. I was relieved that he was fine but I was mad at him for terrifying me.

"I am sorry baby. I just thought of playing a prank on you."

"You scared me. Do you even know..."

I couldn't complete my sentence when tears began to roll down my eyes. And that day I never looked back in life. We were a true couple in every sense. He brought out the girl within me. I had changed for him. He said he liked girls in traditional outfits and in two days I had five ethnic dresses in my wardrobe. Till then I hated, weddings but on his insistence, I had gone to my cousin's marriage. It wasn't that bad either but today even I hate going to weddings. I don't like crowded places.

All this affected my studies. From being a good student, I fell to the average student scale. I was still doing well in Accounts but my Economics was nowhere. I never had time for my studies as all I did was daydream in school, at coaching and at home. Today, I realise he wasn't worth it or was he?

Our Boards went well and both of us were overjoyed to score above 90% but the battle wasn't over. He had his IIT-JEE and I had my CPT. He studied hard for it. I don't know how he never got distracted with all this stuff. Maybe he was more focussed. In a month, we got the news that he had cleared his JEE and had scored a good rank. Everyone expected him to get IIT-Mumbai and he did get into it. Meanwhile, I got admission in SRCC and gave my CPT along with it. I cleared it fairly well. I was onto my next level of CA now.

One problem that we were facing was the long distance that separated us. I was always confident that distance didn't matter in our relationship. And I guess so did he. But things do change with time. With the IIT tag came the drunkard tag too. He had started drinking too much. He even began to take drugs. He was still doing well academically but his attitude towards me had changed. He often abused me and talked to me many a times when he was drunk. This wasn't the Shashank I knew. My Shashank had always been a gentleman. What had happened to him?

And then in one of those drunken moments he wept, saying he had ruined this relationship and it was time to say goodbye. He felt he was not the right guy for me. He didn't want to spoil my life any more. I made him realise that all this wasn't true and he would always be the best guy for me. At that time I thought he was too drunk and that was why he was saying all such rubbish, but there were many truths to unfold or rather many lies to be told.

The next day, on waking up, our break up was first thing he wanted to have. I cried, begged but he was adamant. I made him realise that he couldn't do this and we really loved each other, but my pleas fell on deaf ears. I thought of making him understand things during the Diwali vacations he would have, but he never came to Delhi. Believe me, that was my worst Diwali ever.

And then I called up Vishal, his best friend.

"Hello."

"Hello. May I speak to Vishal?"

"Yes, who's this?"

"Hi! Vishal. This is Priyanka, Shashank's girlfriend."

"Hmm...yes Priyanka," his voice sounded grim. I guess he knew what must be happening in our relationship.

"See, Vishal, I don't think I need to tell you anything. You might know whatever is happening in our life. I need your help. I need you to convince him that I really love him from the core of my heart and our relation still stands strong. We can work out things. I'll manage everything. I just need your help for I know he listens only to you. Please help me out."

"Priyanka, all of us know he has changed. I am still his close friend but he resides in Mumbai and myself in Delhi. My words aren't affective any more. He has his own life and it's his decision. I cannot interfere but for you and your love, I'll try once again. I cannot assure you the good times, but I'll try my level best."

"Okay... I hope you aren't hiding anything from me?" I asked Vishal.

He paused for some time and gave a sigh, "No Priyanka."

"Okay. Till when will you call him?"

"I'll talk to him by afternoon or tonight."

"Okay... I'll call you to check things."

"Yes. I'll let you know. Bye Priyanka."

"Bye!"

❖ ❖ ❖

Things never went well after that. I came to know he had made another girlfriend. The ground beneath me shook heavily. I don't know for how long I cried but I know I fainted in the process of weeping. Thoughts like suicide kept haunting me every moment. I would get tears in my eyes in the middle of lectures and even while hanging out with friends. I stopped going to my favourite coffee shop altogether. I was scared to even pass by the places where we had spent time together. I hated the bench in the park where I used to have telephonic conversations with him every morning and evening. I couldn't believe that all this had actually happened in my life. But, I had no other option. I was just a chapter in his life that had got over. Why had he become the dog in our bond? I always thought I would be the bitch. But man, I had stayed on for such a long time and it hurt to see that everything had been shattered in seconds. May be my blind faith in him had brought this to me.

And one day your ego of having the best man in your life shall break.

Alas! He was in love again but not with me.

Coming out of a breakup wasn't easy for me. There were many sleepless nights and wet pillows but Vishal was there with me always. He had become a good friend with time. We used to meet often as we had common Metro routes. He had been studying BCA at IP University. Till then I had failed miserably at IPCC, the second gateway to getting the C.A. tag. I had by then got interested in Fashion Designing. I had discovered a new found passion within me and I decided to give a last try to IPCC and if I didn't pass, I would give up C.A. That was a different kind of phase. Every friend that I had ignored all this while came into the picture. I spent my maximum time with them and till date I've never had such great time with friends. I had Vishakha and Vishal, the best of friends around me. We had become a well-known trio everywhere. Life was fun, at least externally. Nights were tough though. Vishal had been by my side every time I broke down at night.

❖ ❖ ❖

Shashank says:

I know I did wrong to her. I was always afraid of telling her. I had known it since long that it wasn't love; it was an infatuation for me. I realised it all when I fell for Nitika. I wish I had told her then, but I couldn't gather the courage. I knew she loved me from the core of her heart. She would not have been able to bear this. I knew I was driving her crazy. I was venting my frustration on her. I wish Nitika had come into my life before. She had come but she'd never been so effective on me till Priyanka came. I guess she was slowly getting drawn towards me or maybe she was making sure whether it was just love or another case of infatuation.

I seek her forgiveness, but she doesn't forgive me. I've a big burden on my shoulders. I have committed a sin but I can handle it no longer. May be it would have been better had I stayed with her all the while, keeping her encompassed by my lies, at least she would have been better.

I have lost my best friend for her. Vishal left me, blaming me for her helplessness. I know I am a devil. Because of me, she is in this plight. Vishal said she has fallen into acute depression. Doctors have prescribed high doses of medicine for her. She threw them away that very instant. She was trying to be brave. I can feel the coldness in her fake laughter when she calls me. She calls me almost daily to enquire about my wellbeing. She still cares about me. She puts up a brave front too often these days. She cares but she doesn't show. It isn't out of habit that she calls me; it's out of care. I know it, I've seen her care for long.

Vishal and I had a big fight yesterday. She doesn't know. He caught my collar, saying I had done wrong to her. He doesn't say, but I can see the spark of love for her in his eyes. It's not his fault; anyone can fall in love with a nice girl like Priyanka. But I am feeling a little jealous. I don't love her but I can't digest Vishal's feelings for her. Somehow the match between Priyanka and Vishal sounds weird. If he truly loves her, then I am really happy for them. She deserves a man who loves her unconditionally. I am happy for you, Priyanka and Vishal. I hope one day you guys will forgive me.

"No dumbo, I just can't forget him. Every day I try but I just can't."

Sniff! Sniff!

"Priyanka, please don't cry. You've been going on for fifteen minutes like this. Have mercy on my balance."

"Shut up! Miser. I'll call you up. How many times have I told you to get a better connection that provides good tariff."

"No, no need. I was just saying all this to cheer you up. You know I just can't see you cry."

"See, that is why I call you Dumbo. We are on a phone call, so you can't see me Vishal. You can just hear me."

"I am not Dumbo."

"You are."

"I'm not."

"You are."

"Look, I am really not Dumbo. I am Vishal, okay?"

"Hahaha...You are not Vishal, you are Dumbo."

"Stop it! I am not Vishal, I am Dumbo."

And I burst out laughing, "You've accepted it yourself."

"Thank God. At least that made you laugh. I wish I could keep indulging in such stupidity only to hear your laughter. Smile suits you better. Do you know that you look extremely cute when you smile."

"Really?"

"Yes, Ms. Melodrama. You should always be happy in every circumstance. There'll be many hurdles in your way, but there's always one thing that your enemies can't snatch from you."

"And what is that?"

"Your sweet smile. If you learn to smile in every situation, sadness will run away from you. Got it?"

"Yes Sir."

"And in the first case, why do you have to be sad? He wasn't worth it. He left you for someone else. And you are cute enough to get a good boyfriend. You are just a little fat, a little short, a little less beautiful, a little stupid and a big drama queen."

"Are you actually praising me, dumbo? Can't I get a handsome and loving guy?"

"Well I wouldn't accept your proposal."

"As if I'll ever propose to a guy and that to you. Ugh! I have some standards."

"Excuse me Ma'am, I've quite a number of female fans at college and they say I've got killer eyes. And even in school, half the girls were after me."

"Huh! I am not blind and okay, I agree you've got good looks but you've no brains. Look at yourself. Six feet tall. Who wants a guy like an electric pole?"

"So according to you, having good height is outdated. Which man in the glamour world is short like you? Your Mr. Leonardo isn't and nor is your Shahid Kapoor. Leave it Priyanka, you are just jealous."

"I am not jealous, okay! I like them for their acting skills and super cool looks."

"Yeah... whatever. You are the biggest drama queen I've ever met, *nautanki.*"

"So what? I am what I am and I love the way I am. I don't care about what people think about me. And if someone dares to poke his nose in my affairs, I'll just kick him out of my way."

"Okay...okay, enough Ms. Attitude. I would now suggest you to go and sleep as it's already late. You've classes to attend. C'mon cutie pie, go to sleep."

"Hmmm... even I feel the same. Goodnight dumbo, sweet dreams, take care and thanks a ton."

"Thanks for what?" he asked.

"For being there with me. For being there when I needed you the most," I replied. I had to thank him. No one could sacrifice so much of his time and sleep for just another lonely girl.

"Yes, you just can't sign off without your daily dose of formality. Go to sleep now. Bye!"

"Bye!"

I think the worst mistake a man can ever make is to give another man a chance to make his girl smile. And this was very true in my case. Vishal had earned a good amount of respect in my eyes. He was my saviour and my best friend.

❖ ❖ ❖

Vishal says:

I love her. I love her, truly, madly and deeply. I am unable to express my feelings but I do love her. I'll never make her cry. I'll never let a single tear fall from her eyes. For her, I fought with Shashank. I hope she never finds out. Both of us are sailing in the same boat. The only difference is I lost my love, Ayesha two years back and she has been lonely since the past few months. We need to move on in life.

When I saw her break up with Shashank, I saw her castle of dreams collapse. It hasn't been easy for her, I know. I've been through all this. And I don't want her to go through the same pain as I did. I knew about Nitika since day one and I had pestered Shashank to tell her the truth but he never came out with it. Thankfully she came to know about Nitika after a month of their break up. It wasn't too sudden for her. That night she had cried her heart out and that very instant I resolved to try to bring all the happiness in her life.

Priyanka is rough from outside only. But from inside, she is the most beautiful girl I've ever met. She has a heart of gold and I guess that is why people easily play with her heart. I don't want to see her cry again. I am ready to wait for her as I know it takes time for wounds to heal. I know she'll be back to her normal self soon and the day she starts feeling for me, I'll propose to her and this proposal is going to be for ever; a promise to be by her side lifelong. I wish I could tell you Priyanka, I love you. Your Dumbo really loves you.

Another sleepless night has gone by and yet again a new day has arrived. I thank God for the night that has passed by. This lessens a night from my life without you. Passing the day in your absence is an arduous task. How am I going to spend my life without you? Where did I go wrong? I wish I knew what made you leave me? Were all the promises a lie? Why did you go away from me? Wasn't my love enough for you? What was so different in Nitika's love that you dropped me from your life?

I picked up my pen and penned a poetry that reflected my thoughts and the pain that was still fresh. It had been a while since Shashank had left but the wounds hadn't healed yet. It hurt.

It Still Hurts...

It's been long since you left me,

It's been ages since I had a talk with you,

It's been months since I last saw you,

It's been long since I touched you,

It's been ages since I hugged you,

It's been months since I kissed you,

It's been long since I sat next to you,

It's been months since I ate ice cream with you,

It's been ages since we studied together,

It's been long since I laughed like I used to before,

It's been months since I gave time to myself,

It's been ages since I cried,

My smile left me,

My tears have also left me.

My emotions left me,

Since the day you left me.

Everything which was mine left me.

It's been long... but it still hurts...

It still hurts to be away from you,

It still hurts to sit alone,

It still hurts to have silent days

It still hurts to have quiet nights.

still hurts to be myself again.

It still hurts

It still hurts

It still hurts...

❖ ❖ ❖

Nothing's gonna change my love for you

You ought to know by now how much I love you

One thing you can be sure of

I'll never ask for more than your love.

My cell phone rang. Since the past year, my ringtones had become less noisy. Dumbo calling, it shouted out.

"Hello," I said as I picked up his call.

"Good morning, Ms. Melodrama. Woken up?"

"Yeah... long time back."

"Did you even sleep?"

"I did. Chill, man."

"Okay. I just asked casually. So tell me, what's the plan?"

"Plan? What plan?"

"Today's plan. Are we meeting today and are you bunking college today also?"

"Hmm... I don't know."

"Priyanka, you have to move on in life. It doesn't stop here. Start leading a normal life. You know college days are among the best times of your life. Don't miss them for a guy who didn't value your love. Don't spoil your present and future for your past. You are not the only one who has been through this. We've all been through this. Learn something from Vishakha. She has a break up every month or two. Even I had a break up with my girlfriend and it doesn't hurt any more. And that's only because I want to help myself and I wanted to get out of it. Nothing can help you till you yourself want to get out of this misery. And stupid, if I can do it, so can you, for you, are so much better than me.

"Oh! No, please don't start crying again. Priyanka, please, please don't cry," pleaded Vishal.

"Yes, I am not crying. I'll not weep for him anymore. Everyone goes through it. This is what you said. But I can't. It was a shock for me. My whole world has been shattered. My dreams, my happiness, my world...all have come crashing down in a second. You say even you went through all this but somewhere, you had the hint of your relation going awry, but I didn't know all this. Shashank was always talking so lovingly to me that I couldn't even sense that things were going wrong. He never talked about things going through rough times, he never told me that he had a problem with me. We didn't even have a single fight in such a long span; no, wait, we quarrelled once. Yes, in such a big time period we fought once, so how could I even imagine that all this would be happening in my life?"

"Hello... Vishal, are you there?" I guess I often rendered him tongue tied due to so much of talking.

"Umm...yes I am listening to whatever you are saying and to an extent you are right," he replied in a grim tone.

"I am sorry if I said something wrong," I said, feeling low.

"No sweets, you are always right. It's alright I can understand. Now get up, you lazy bones. It's 8 a.m already. One hour will be enough for you to get done with your make up," he said, trying to tease me.

"Excuse me, what was the last sentence you just said? Makeup and Priyanka are always miles apart. I am not like your ex. I don't take more than fifteen minutes to get ready," I roared.

"Haha! That's because you don't bathe."

"I was talking about getting ready after taking the bath. Huh!" I hate to admit but this idiot will always get fun by teasing me.

"You are a shame in the name of SRCC. Just look at you and the rest of the girls."

"I don't like being the eye candy."

"That wasn't the case when I first saw you a year back. You looked prettier then; you still do but the charm and spark from your face seem to have vanished."

"Thank you. If I look boring these days, it's all because of your bastard friend," I said in exasperation.

"One tip: You always feel good if you look good. Mark my words."

"Oh! Really? Inspirational speaker, see you in 45 minutes at the Metro station. Don't be late. I don't like waiting for random guys," I said in full attitude.

"Yeah, whatever my drama queen. See ya, bye!"

"Bye Dumbo and yes, I wrote a poem last night; will show you today."

"Another heartbreak musing, I know but I'll read as I know you write beautifully.

"Hmm... Okay, bye!"

"Bye!"

Dumbo's words made me look at my reflection in the mirror. What had I done to myself? When Shashank had come into picture, I had turned girlie instantly and after his departure, I had become so dull. Earlier I took extra pain to look good, now I didn't even pay attention to combing my hair properly. And that day, after almost an era, I actually got dressed properly. And needless to say, I got some great compliments from friends and certainly from Dumbo and Vishakha.

I had finally decided to dump Shashank from my mind and who else would get to know about it apart from Dumbo and Vishaka? As usual, we three was sitting in CCD and having a chat when I divulged the news. "Guys, there is a good news for you," I spoke cheerfully.

"What? Are you pregnant?"

Who else could have given such a stupid response? It was our very own Vishakha. I looked straight into her eye and they both burst out laughing.

"Shut up! This one's better."

"Now, break the suspense drama queen." That was Dumbo addressing me.

"Okay...okay. I have finally decided to throw the bastard into trash and give a chance to new ones."

"Wow! This is going to be so exciting, Priyanka. Looking out for a suitable guy for you. I am so happy," squealed Vishakha, hugging me tightly. She knew I hated her extra cajoling but just could not get rid of it.

I had expected the same response from Dumbo but he just smiled.

"Hello...I am not going out seriously with any guy. It'll only be harmless flirting. I miss being committed when you get to ride with your boyfriend and going on a date is something I am really looking forward to these days."

"Ooo..lala.. someone is going to give me competition."

"C'mon Vish, that can never be. I can never surpass your number of boyfriends."

"It's party time. Be ready at eight tonight. We are going to Agni. This will also help us find some *chikna munda* for you," Vishakha spoke.

"Okay, done. Dumbo, you coming, right? Don't say there's an appointment with the doc today for aunty," I said.

"Yes I am coming. I am free today."

"Yay! By the way Dumbo, how is aunty?" I asked out of concern.

"She is better. After Dad's demise, I never saw her as hale and hearty as she used to be."

"It hasn't been easy for her. Losing your love is tough and who can understand this better than me? Shashank and I dated for some time but it has been too tough for me to get over it and just think about her. He was her life, her life partner. They had been married for years and being snatched away from your love forever is too rude. I can at least talk to Shashank when I want. I know he is happy without me but come to think of it, she has to pass the rest of her life without his presence. By the way, you know what Dumbo? Sometimes I wonder where did the brains of your family go? You don't even have a pinch of their grey matter." That was me with another random rambling, jumping, from one topic to other.

"I thought I should do something different. Everybody is a doctor in our family, so there should be an exception, a black sheep in the family. Dr. Vishal Bhargava doesn't suit me."

"An easy way to get out of problems, right Vishal? You should certainly start figuring out your life. You are always clueless as to what you have to do. Tell me one thing, why did you go for BCA?" And can you even think of it, this was being said by Vishakha, who herself was clueless about things in her life.

"I took it because my ex girlfriend also took this course, plus I didn't want to get into engineering and I have been good at coding since long."

"Wow! What great reasons! Anyway, time to pack up. Be sure to pick Priyanka from home," I saw Vish wink at him but I didn't get it and I was too pre-occupied to think that there was something cooking between them and about which I was unaware.

I was getting ready in the evening when I heard a car honk at my doorstep.

"Pia, get ready soon. Vishal is here," Mom called.

"Yes Mom."

It was just 7:40 p.m. What was the need to come so early? I had taken special care to look good. I was wearing a dark purple coloured one-piece with stilettos that were hard to carry after a long time. But then, all in all, I looked good for my Dad stood there gazing at me and saying, "My Angel has grown big and is looking beautiful as ever."

"Look, there is no point saying you are looking like a clown today because mistakenly you are looking too good today. Remember to stay away from boys, avoid their comments and better not reply to any unknown random guy. Got it." This was my younger brother giving me advice. And I long waited for a compliment from Dumbo but he didn't say anything. He just kept staring at me, sometimes smiling and sometimes giving some weird expression. And no doubt, he was looking handsome as always.

As I sat in his car beside him, there was a different vibe that I had never felt before. "How come you brought your car today? You always bring your soul mate, your bike," I asked.

"This is to protect a pretty lady from filthy eyes."

"Oh! Thank you," I smiled as I said this.

We obviously had a great night that day. As I entered 'Agni', an unknown vibe entranced me, telling me from within that life had still not lost its zeal.

"Okay, so here we go. You are having tequila shots today."

Yes, it was Vishakha.

"No way. I've just had beer till date and I'm certainly not going to try tequila in one shot."

"Do you want to move on?" she asked in an infuriated tone.

"Yes."

"It'll help you. You know why? Because Shashank always restrained you from trying alcohol and you so wanted to taste it. You are not going to become an alcoholic in one night. You just have to give it a try."

Vishakha is a cunning girl. She made me do it by reasoning out about Shashank and no way could I refuse for I had pledged to keep him off my mind. And that day finally, I had the first drink of my life. People begin from beer to vodka but I directly jumped to tequila shots after beer and oh my God, it had such a weird taste but before I could think about anything, it had already gone inside and taken control over me. I felt a different kind of feeling gush inside. I found myself wrapped around with new energy and enthusiasm. Yes, it was finally time to dance my heart out.

There were many who came forward to talk to me but I danced my heart out. I saw a spark of jealousy in Vishal's eyes many a times when I talked to random guys.

Vishal came back to drop me. He had been silently smiling all through the way while I was jabbering away. I didn't quite question him on this, but it was a little weird watching him silently listen to me. Romantic songs were being played in the background and there was nothing new in it as Dumbo loved to hear romantic songs and none of us could beat him on his knowledge of Hindi music. Later I did come to know that he had taken extra efforts to play the best of songs that night in his car.

Things between Dumbo and me changed pretty soon. We would chat longer and tried to spend most of the time together. Earlier we were always accompanied by Vishakha but the mighty trio had turned to a duet. I don't know why she herself backed out from all these outings. Whenever I would call her for a hangout, she'd give the excuse of being busy or going on a date with some random guy. Vish never gave a damn to her boyfriends although circumstances had changed. I didn't give a second thought to all this, as I always felt that people do change with time. She would still hear my stories every day; our meetings had become less freqnent anyway. I often wonder if it was a conscious decision or was it due to the turn of events.

❖ ❖ ❖

Just another Monday morning.

10:00 a.m.

Café Coffee Day, New Delhi.

"Vish, I really don't know what to do?"

"See Vishal, you don't have to lose heart. She is hurt badly. We all know that and it'll take time for the wound to heal."

"The point is not this, Vishakha. I am worried whether she'll ever be able to fall in love with anybody else."

"She will fall in love again and not just someone, she will definitely fall for you."

"I sometimes wonder if I'm really suitable for her or not. She deserves a good man, someone who'll actually take care of her and understand her feelings."

"You've been with her when she actually needed someone and honestly, you supported her more than I could ever do."

"You know Vish, I always felt that life was being unfair with her but this time I want to give her all the happiness of the world. I want to return to her all the time she lost because of my best friend. I want to turn her pain into joy. I love the way she laughs, I just can't see her sad or staying aloof from the world. I love her and I'm telling you that even if she rejects me, I'll wait for her."

"And that is what I want for her. She is the best and I want the best man for her and what better can it be than to watch my two best friends in love."

"O! Wow! Am I your bestie?"

"Yes and I think she has started liking you. I mean she doesn't say anything but if given time, she will be yours. She will love you for what you have been to her."

"Vishakha, I've always played pranks on you but today I heartily want to thank you for the support you give me every time I feel apprehensive about losing the girl I love."

"Always welcome. Treat me to some good coffee today. It's time to repay my goodness,"

"Sure girl, what'll you have?"

I had finally failed in IPCC again. And this was the last time I was giving a chance to C.A. Frankly speaking, the third failure in IPCC didn't matter much for I was fed up of C.A. You burn your ass off for months and shit is what you get in return. The pass percentage is even less than one per cent. What do the C.A. institute people think of themselves? Don't they think about how much cash and effort are lost for this exam and still they do not pass us? I was finally done with love, C.A and bullshit. I knew where to head to. My new found interest was Fashion Designing and it was time to work on it. You never know when life changes for you.

"Priyanka, what exactly do you want to do?"Dad asked me angrily.

I knew that from inside he was feeling tired and betrayed. His daughter wasn't able to pass a stupid exam, the exam in which he had topped in his region. He took it as his own failure. I was feeling sorry for him, more than I ever felt for myself. "Dad, I've tried umpteen times and I've always given my best. Unfortunately I haven't been able to find success and I don't wish to continue with this anymore. If you feel I should give it a try again, I'll give it again but now I am really done with C.A."

"Are you sure?"

"Yes."

"What will you do then?" he asked, still unable to believe what I had said. I had once been so enthusiastic about this profession and now I was ready to let it go.

I dreaded saying those words but it had to come some day. I gulped water and said, "Fashion Designing."

"What? Are you crazy? I thought you would want to do some course in accountancy or Company Secretariat or may be M.B.A. but you want to do a stupid course. Mrs. Preeti Bajaj, please put some brain into your daughter's head," he said to mom, baffled and angry.

I really don't know why do all husbands of this world have this habit of blaming their wives when they are scolding their kids? Okay, he wasn't blaming Mom for anything, but what was the point of asking her to add some grey matter into my empty head? And like always my super clever Mom didn't interfere in the arguments between a Dad and daughter. I knew she would have a discussion with him before going to bed.

"Dad, I am not fit for jobs like these. I wasn't even sixteen when I took up commerce. I saw you as my idol and thought I would study what you had studied and help you out in office but choices change with time and today at 21, I know what I am meant for. I am not for audit, I am meant for a creative field."

"*Three Idiots* has brought havoc in the life of parents. They show crap and you people blindly follow it. It was a movie and that is why he became a famous and successful photographer. This is reality, not some stupid movie going on. Not every fashion designer becomes Ritu Kumar. Talk some sense, Priyanka."

"Dad, I might be crossing my limits today. I've never argued with you like this ever, but today I wish to do something that I really love. I know there'll be no one to support me in this field, no one to back me up but whatever I will be, it'll be just because of my personal effort and one day I promise, Mom won't go for a Ritu Kumar dress she'll go for mine. And you said we're following crap on TV but I am saying this with all true feelings just like he said it in '*Three Idiots*.' Whatever I'll be, I will never blame you for what I am doing. Dad, have some belief in me. I will make you proud."

Dad looked at me and somewhere I could see acceptance in his eyes but all he said was, "I will think over it. Let's have dinner."

I ate the least that night and didn't even sleep for a second. Vishal called me up to ask what had happened. I narrated the whole incident to him and he kept comforting me. I was getting restless and all I did that night was drink water and piss.

"Dumbo, I am so scared. I don't know if Dad would approve of my idea or not. I can feel those butterflies in my stomach."

"Which one, red or yellow?"

"Shut up. Why do you always have to be funny?" I said, getting agitated.

"I just want you to get over this restlessness and sleep."

"You know what? You are really sweet, Dumbo."

"Thank you. Now just relax and go to bed. It'll do you good. And don't forget to give us a treat in the evening tomorrow."

"Treat? What for?" I asked.

"For not clearing IPCC the third time. You've come into my category and for getting uncle's permission. I am sure he will agree to your decision. Any parents can do anything for their children and he loves you. Tears are the last thing he wants to see in your eyes."

"Really?" I asked for assurance from his side.

"Yes. Don't worry."

This is what I loved in Vishal. He was always there to provide me the positive energy whenever I seemed to have lost it. He was my own Robin Sharma. I felt as if some good deeds were being repaid in the form of such a good friend. He had become an indispensible part of my life.

We hung up the call in the middle of the night for we both had run out of balance. I tried to sleep but I couldn't, however hard I tried. I kept on tossing and turning in my bed and finally I plugged in my headphones to listen to Lady Gaga. Everybody hates her but I love her for her whacky style. She has the guts to be different and no amount of criticism seems to make her disappointed. The remaining night went off with *Alejandro* (and if you are wondering what I just said it's a song by Lady Gaga and I love the liveliness in its music).

I woke up red eyed and the first question Mom asked me was whether I had actually slept all night or not. We were having breakfast but unlike always, everyone was silent. I looked at my Mom and then gave a look to my bro. He in turn began staring at Dad. God, what was he doing?

"Umm... Dad, what are the plans for today?" my younger bro asked.

"I have some work. I need to talk to some interior decorators."

"Why?" he quizzed.

"We need to set up a small boutique for your sister as that is going to be her workstation. As soon as she graduates, we will get her admitted to NIFT. In the meanwhile, she can also intern under your Mom's friend, who happens to be a designer."

I went numb. I couldn't believe Dad had approved of my decision and not only that, he had gone out of the way to help me out. I was happy beyond limits and ran to hug Dad.

"Thank you so much, Dad. You are the best Dad in the whole world."

"I know sweetheart and we always want to see this smile on your face. And for this, you'll have to thank your Mom. She made me understand things even to the point that it would save my bank balance as she would wear your creations from now onwards,"

Dad said, laughing and I hugged both of them. And I don't need to mention that my brother couldn't tolerate so much of love being poured over me but he had to join in. The breakfast table had suddenly turned into a celebration moment. My Mom had tears in her eyes. I guess every Mom gets those tears of joy.

The first thing I did after that was to call Dumbo. "Get ready for some party, dude. It's a 'yes' from Dad's side. Let me take Vishakha on conference. I just can't tell you how happy I am," I rattled off in excitement.

We celebrated the whole day, from Dilli Haat to Saket, we roamed about everywhere. We went for a movie that day itself, but this time we sat in the corner and Vishakha went to sit with some other friend she met there accidentally. I sometimes feel she did it purposely. The movie was going in full swing. In between I often felt as if Dumbo was watching me more than the movie but I erased that thought away. But changes do come in life. The last scene of the movie showed the hero putting the ring on the heroine's finger and I felt Dumbo holding my hand tightly.

I looked at him. Even in the darkness I could see his eyes speak of something. It wasn't clear but I could make out that it was not a friendly touch; it was a touch that stated his love. I kept on staring at him and silly me didn't even ask him to remove his hand. The movie ended and both of us sat silent. It was as if suddenly the loudest channel had gone mute. We couldn't stay mum even for a second but that day we said nothing to each other on the whole way back home. And that day he didn't speed his bike after entering Noida. I walked in without saying a word to him. Needless to say, we didn't talk that night and the next day.

I sent him a forwarded message after two days of silence. He sent one in return. And we played this game of sending forwarded messages to each other for around forty minutes. My phone rang. I saw that Vishakha was calling. I hadn't told her anything about it yet and at this time, I didn't want to talk to her. I just wanted to stay alone but I had no chance. If I didn't pick up her call, she'd call home in a fraction of seconds.

"Silly woman, what the hell are you doing since the past forty minutes? Can't you say something else rather than sending stupid messages?"

"What?" I asked shocked as to how she had come to know about this? But then there was nothing hidden between all three of us. Vishal must have told her everything.

"Yes. I've got bored of watching his stupid expressions and your idiotic messages. If you like him, say 'yes' and if you don't, then go to hell."

"Vishakha, this is not a game."

"Yes girl, that is what I want to tell you. This is not a game that you'll keep on playing with Vishal's sentiments. He is ready to wait for you all his life but that doesn't mean you will keep him on hold till your wounds are healed. You keep on crying for that asshole and lose a good guy in the process."

I kept silent and let out a sigh in the middle.

"Get some grey matter, woman. He loves you but is afraid of telling you anything just because it will hurt you. What better guy would you ever find? I think you should come over to Mandi House. We're sitting at Costa Coffee."

"Now?" I asked with a surprised expression on my face. Honestly speaking, I didn't want to go there and have a discussion but I had no option as Vishakha would have forced me to come anyway.

"Yes, it's an order and you have to follow it. It won't take more than half an hour or do you want me to send Vishal over to your place?"

"No, that's fine. I will come."

I got up from my couch that I hadn't left since the morning. The way from my home to Mandi House had me in the most disturbed state. Believe me, I wasn't so disturbed even when I gave my second attempt of IPCC. I didn't know if I should say 'yes' to Vishal or stay single. I was not sure if I would be able to face him again.

I entered Costa Coffee with peculiar thoughts in my mind. I didn't have the courage to even glance at Vishal. I waved at Vishaka and sat down, trying not to look into his eyes. I tried looking at him through a side glance. He looked all worked up. His eyes were red just like mine; his shirt wasn't ironed and he kept on shaking his legs as I kept on beating my nails on the table.

"I will take leave now. You guys can have a discussion over it and let me know the verdict," said Vishakha, picking up her bag. How could she leave me alone at this juncture? I regretted having come and I gave a 'I will see you bitch' look to Vishakha.

After she left, I kept on fidgeting in my place, sometime trying to make my hair or adjust my bangles. He was still shaking his legs.

My phone beeped and it was Vishal. He knew that it would be tough for me to speak. *Hey, how are you?*

It was my turn to reply so I did.

I am good. You?

Me too.

Priyanka, I wanted to say something.

What?

If it's not okay with you, I can get over it. We can still be friends.

Dumbo, I respect your love but the point is I never gave it a thought that we could be a couple. You've been my pillar of strength. You helped me come out of my depression at Shashank's betrayal. I'll always be grateful to you but I really don't know if I am ready for a relationship or not. I've failed miserably in one and getting into another would be too early.

Hmm... I understand Priyanka. I respect your feelings and I am really sorry for my misdeed that day. I was overcome by emotions.

That's okay, Dumbo, you need not be sorry.

Priyanka, before you leave, I just want to say that I really love you.

I wish I could say what you want to hear. Bye, Shashank.

Oh no, what had I just typed? Had I just called him Shashank? I corrected the sentence and sent him. *I wish I could say what you may have wanted to hear. Bye, Vishal!*

Our hangouts had become less now and I was too busy with designing my workstation. Even if we did, we silently drank coffee. The firehouse of laughter had been burnt down. We still exchanged forwarded message with each other three times a day but our conversation had reduced to 'Hello' and 'How are you?'

About a week later, I received a message from Vishal stating that he was tired with this strained friendship and therefore he was leaving Delhi. There was a need to panic. Where was he going? And what was the point of doing such stuff? I called up Vishakha to find out what was up with him. Even she didn't know about this so. I instantly called him up.

"Where the hell do you think you are going?"

"Pune."

"And why so?" I burst out at him.

"Need a change, that's it."

"Look, there is no need to do all this. I really don't understand boys. Half of them ditch and some like you leave everything for a girl. Just because a girl has rejected your proposal doesn't mean that it is the end of life and it doesn't mean she'll never reconsider you."

"What? What was the last sentence you just said?"

"I just said that there are always chances of a girl reconsidering a proposal. I can't surely say in our case but even if I rejected you doesn't mean you will leave your best friend. The girl who doesn't care for you doesn't deserve all this. But friends will always be there with you. Let's just go and party and forget the bitch."

He smirked and just said, "It's not that easy, mate. Nevertheless, you guys enjoy. My flight leaves in four hours. I need to hang up your call."

I sent him a message: *Why are you doing this, dumbo?*

He replied after an hour: *To make myself forget you.*

He went away, leaving us alone. We didn't talk about him much but we missed him. To me it felt as if there was a vacuum in my life. I just couldn't imagine life without him. I wanted him back. It is said that distance helps you grow fonder and this did happen in our case. One week without him felt like ages. We were in regular touch through messages and exactly after thirty days, I sent him a special message: *I like you dumbo*

I really don't know why I said this but it was something close to what I felt. I didn't love him but I did like him.

What? Are you serious?

I knew he would say this. *Yes I am. I do like you. I don't know if I love you or not, but I do like you. I love the way you love me and I am glad I have found a man like you. And if there's someone like you in my life, I don't mind falling in love, given some time. I just want to stay by your side. Life has been too bad without you since the past month and all I need is your presence to make my life better. Please come back.*

It took twenty minutes for me to type this message. It was tough to make sense. Thank God I didn't have to speak all this in front of him or else I would have got cold feet. I always fall short of words.

I really don't know if I am dreaming or not, but I do want to believe what you say. I have been dying to hear this from you. I just need a chance from your side. God, why did you take so long? I had been so depressed all these days; couldn't even eat properly. I didn't even have a look at any of the girls around just because of you.

Alas! Men will be men. He is such an idiot; he is regretting the fact that he couldn't eye chicks. Loser!

Ha ha ha! Idiot, now go and enjoy. Party out with friends tonight and come back within two days after you're done with your personal sightseeing.

I don't need to. I'll be back to our Delhi soon. Till then, you take care of yourself, baby.

Does a boy change this way when a girl enters his life? And hold on, he called me 'baby'. Man! It's going to be tough. Suddenly I became his baby from the super troublesome drama queen. But whatever the case was, he would always be my Dumbo.

I instantly called Vish and told her that I had patched up things with Dumbo. He would be coming soon and we would party big time.

Haa! Mission accomplished finally. I had got my best friend back and we three were back with a bang. I felt immeasurable pleasure and delight engulf me after a long span of time. At last, I had a sound sleep and didn't even once get interrupted by stupid thoughts. And that day I came to learn the contentment and value of a sound sleep.

I didn't know whether I should call myself single or committed. Even though I was clueless as to what was happening around was right or wrong, I was happy that things had finally got over regarding Shashank and I could be happy with someone else. The chapter of Shashank was closed and I was ready to start my life with my best friend. Both of us went to fetch Vishal to the airport. Clever Vishakha asked me to hide and I noticed his eyes were searching for me.

"Where is she?" he quizzed Vishakha.

"She didn't come."

"Why?"

"She realised that she had done wrong to herself by pretending things, so she doesn't have the courage to face you now."

"What the fuck!"

Before Vish could utter more nonsense, I came into the picture, smiling at him and he knew I had gone nowhere. I walked towards him to shake hands and exchanged a warm hug.

"You are looking beautiful, Priyanka," he whispered in my ears while the hug was on.

They asked me to move on in the car and a few minutes later, I had flowers in my hand, the most beautiful combination of yellow and red roses. And I knew this relation was going to be fun. Having your best buddy as your partner is the best thing that could have happened to me.

We planned an outing that night and it couldn't have been better than being proposed by Vishal in front of my best friend Vishakha. The occupants at McDonalds saw him proposing to me.

With a red rose in his hand and kneels down, he recited:

Till now we had been just friends
But now things are going to change.
I'll never stop being your best buddy
I just want to get promoted to the man of your life.
I may not be good at expressing well
But all I want to say is...
I promise to stay by your side forever.
I promise to not let tears wet your eyes,
I promise to wake you up every morning,
I promise to be by your side every night,
I promise to make your days brighter,
I promise to make your life more colourful,
I promise to do every little thing that makes you happy.
I promise to eat ice cream with you daily,
I promise to pick you up from office daily,
I promise to have dinner out every weekend,
I promise to work hard for you,
I promise to give you the best of living,
I promise to never keep you waiting,
I promise to be with you forever and ever
I promise to love you till death does us part.

I was awestruck and a little emotional too. After a long time, happiness had knocked on my door. I was scared of embracing it, afraid of losing it again but as the saying goes, every cloud has a silver lining may be this time things would go well. May be I should take the glass as half filled rather than half empty. And Shashank's departure had not only given me a best friend but also a boyfriend. Who knows I might as well stay with him all my life?

Life was back on track now. I started from home to catch the Metro but I always had Vishal waiting ten steps away from home. He didn't want my family to get suspicious of him. We rarely attended classes and even if I did, I always had Vishal waiting for me at the college gate after my classes got over. I felt proud to get compliments from my gang of girlies.

"Oh My God, you've got a hot guy for yourself. I wish even I had such a handsome boy by my side," Rashi didn't forget to say it aloud.

"Hey Priyanka, your boyfriend has come. Don't keep him waiting," Aditi would also leave no stone unturned in letting all know.

And then there were rave reviews as well.

"Since the past six months, we've been watching just one guy with you. Aren't you bored of him? Or you aren't getting another one?" the always haughty and especially averse to me Ishika commented many a times.

"Look, Priyanka's driver has arrived. Let's go girls."

"So are you coming to this party that Ishika is throwing? Wait, I just forgot, you must be busy with your one and only boyfriend."

And I happily ignored them for I knew there were always going to be negative views with positive feedback. Life had changed with time and soon I was up with my own store. I named it 'Bianca', the Italian version of my name. The opening ceremony was fun and of course the credit went to Dad. I loved the place that was flooded with orders, especially from college mates. Girls with whom I had never even interacted in class also dropped by my store and praised my creative skill. I had earned quite a lot of fame in the college campus. Vish, Dumbo and I spent a lot of happy moments there, eating homemade pizzas together. Our Facebook profile was flooded with pictures of togetherness. People from every nook and corner came to know about our relation. Shashank too came to know and the day I changed my relationship status on facebook, he called me up. I let the phone ring not knowing how to respond but something within me told that I should pick up this call as I had not committed a crime by getting committed again.

"So you guys are a couple now?" he asked roughly.

"Yes."

"Good to know that my ex girlfriend is now my ex best friend's present girlfriend. You guys are wonderful. Don't you people understand the true meaning of any relation?" he asked in a bitter tone.

I knew he was drunk and the alcohol had taken over his tongue.

"Shashank, at least you shouldn't be talking about the value of relationships. Things never mattered to you, whether it was me, our relation or your friendship with Vishal. What matters to you is your own happiness, your own enjoyment, your own selfish requirements, your vodka and your girl. Why are you interfering in my life now? Thank you so much for causing havoc into my life; thank you for leaving me so that I could get a man like Vishal. Thanks a ton. Now please leave," I said, going red with anger.

"You are a bitchy slut, that's it," he shouted at me.

"And you are a fucking bastard. Go to hell. Goodbye." Saying so, I hung up the call in anger and threw my phone in disgust. There had always been an intense rivalry between Shashank and my cell phone. They always seem to have a never ending stimuli and response relation. The moment I talked to Shashank, anger would swell up within me and I would instantly throw away my phone. Within the time span he had left me, I had broken three cell phones. I hoped to use this mobile for a longer span of time. I called up Vishal and narrated the whole incident. He asked me to calm down and forget all the crap. Shashank's number went into my reject list then and there. Peace entered my life till he would call me back again with a new number. I didn't give a heck to him. I hated him to the core of my heart. I slept peacefully, recalling the protective words attired by Dumbo. He was certainly my angel.

The mornings began with Vishal's wakeup call and nights went in chatting with him about everything. Our talks were never too romantic but we loved chatting for hours on stupid topics. We gelled like a house on fire. And finally, Dumbo brought a new SIM and cheaper night rates which really helped us save our pocket money. Many a times when I called Dumbo, his cell would be received by his Mom and I really wondered why she disliked me calling him in the evening? Calling him any time of the day and even at 9 p.m. was okay but my call at six would always elicit in weird responses from her. It was a daily ritual to call him to inquire if he had reached home safely or not. He always forgot but I never did. In the meanwhile, I designed some chic apparel for Dumbo as well. We were soon given the tag of the coolest couple. I loved riding his bike, yes with time I had even learnt how to drive his bike.

We were heading to Gurgaon when I first tried my hand on his bike. How can I ever forget the moment? That was the first time he gave a peck on my cheek. The city of Gurgaon is awesome and that day I tried my hand on salsa for the first time in public. Till now I had just practiced Salsa with Vish as my partner but that day I first experienced the heat of the dance. We returned with desires burning within us. And that was the first time, I actually had a 'love topped up with lust' talk with him. And today I thank my stars for not going ahead with him.

The winter season is all about wrapping yourself in the arms of your beloved. The peak of the season is at New Year and our college friends didn't get any other time to chill out in Manali than this.

"You are coming Priyanka?" Shivangi, my batchmate asked.

"No, never. Are you nuts? It'll be freezing cold out there?"

"That's the joy of enjoying winters, snowfall and mountains. What an awesome scene would it be!"

"I am not coming, that's final. I don't care about the snowfall."

"Priyanka, this will be our last outing together. After this, who knows where we all might be? So c'mon, just pack your bags and don't forget to bring Vishal along."

"Heya guys, what's up! Where are you guys planning to go?" Vishal entered the scene and I knew I wouldn't be able to argue any more.

"Vishal, we all are planning to go for an outing and your madam is not ready. Only you can help. Just imagine, New Year at Manali would be so amazing and adventurous," Shivangi blabbered.

"Wow! Hi five Shivangi. This is a great idea. And of course she is coming. You guys chill out. Just go and shop for yourself."

Everyone dispersed and we just looked at each other. He gave me a smile. I smiled back and ran into his arms. This New Year was going to be fun. This was the effect of Vishal on me that he really didn't have to say anything. We often understood without speaking out directly to each other. I now accepted that his school friends were right he really had killer eyes. I wonder what is with me and my boyfriends. Shashank and Vishal, both had the power to make things happen through their eyes. Meanwhile Vishakha and I shopped for hours to get the best dress for the New Years eve and all Vishal could say was, "Can't you girls please do this faster?"

And we always answered, "No."

Finally the day arrived. We packed ourselves in jackets and gloves and set out for the journey to Manali. And like every Bollywood mother, my Mom said, "Son, do take care of my daughter."

I kept on irritating Vishal with this dialogue all through the journey. Later in the evening, sleep took over and the remaining journey went in resting my head on his shoulders something that can be total bliss for any girl. He hugged me tightly as it was turning cold and I never felt better than this. We reached all tired and sleepy waiting eagerly to jump on our beds. We had booked a cottage on rent and it was big enough to accommodate our group of ten.

As we began moving to our rooms after dinner, Vishal held my hands and said, "Aren't we going to stay in one room?"

"No way. Help yourself with Trisha's boyfriend," I said, grinning hard throwing the pillow at him. It was great to see his expression, a mixture of naughtiness and dejection at being unable to get his wants fulfilled.

The camp fire, champagne, lots of food to eat, an array of chit chat and games, everything constituted our New Year. Soon all of them went inside to the grooves of DJ and both of us were left alone. The cold winds blew hard but I didn't feel them. A hot desire was building fire within me. We sat so close that I could hear his breath clearly, our heart beats mounting and hand in hand, we kept looking at each other. I had never seen this spark in his eyes tinged with love. There was just silence which now had become our medium of conversation. His eyes wanted something from me but was I ready for it? The way he looked at me made me self-conscious and I don't know why but I lowered my eyes. I guess he understood my reply. It was becoming difficult to react properly. My lips had become dry and I couldn't help but notice how muscular he looked. The fireworks were playing games with us. We came closer and hugged each other tightly. Clasped in his arms, I came to know about the value of a man in a woman's life. I closed my eyes to let him dominate the act. His lips touched my cheeks and before I could react, our lips met. I could feel something wet on my lower lip. Gradually I felt the tongue movement and soon I was in the process of what we refer for 'smooch.' I don't know for how long we kissed but it felt like eternity. When I finally came back to my senses, I realised I had just had the first kiss of my life. I got up from my place, smiled at him and ran away.

And don't you think I ran away to make him come after me or to rejoice at not being a kiss virgin any more. I ran into the washroom, washed my mouth umpteen times and gargled ten times. How can people say it's sensuous? Man, tasting someone else's saliva is so yuck. I remembered Ron responding to his first kiss with Hermoine as 'wet' in Harry Potter. And yes it was wet; it was pure stupidity. Why do you have to do such an *ugh* thing to show your love? It was annoying and nauseating. I used Colgate Plax and had a lot of mouth fresheners to prevent myself from vomiting. And how the hell was I going to face Vishal?

The rest of the visit went by smoothly but I never let that smooch happen again on that trip. I was happy with the peck on the cheeks and a hot kiss on neck was also acceptable but not a smooch. Hell, no! He tried hard but I always responded with a strict no. I sometimes wonder why men are just born to enjoy favours from us? And then I reason out that men will be men and all men are dogs. Oh! Wait a second. They aren't dogs for dogs are meant to be faithful; they are actually pigs. I guess I am inciting the male fraternity. And both the genders can never think on the same lines for men are from Mars and women are from Venus. I better leave this discussion as this is always a never ending argument and I really do not want to invite danger at my place.

After the Manali trip, Vishal tried planning many a trip to Agra, Chandigarh and blah-blah but I never gave in to them. I was happy roaming around with him in Delhi and enjoyed his company to the core. I had befriended his friends too, Shubham and a very jovial personality Veeru Paaji. They were a lovely bunch and were always there to help us out in every possible way. When Vishal had to suddenly go to Chennai for his mother's treatment, Veeru Paaji was given the responsibility to see if I had everything that I needed. Shubham was asked to go behind me all the way from college back home for Vishal always felt that I might run into someone while riding my scooty. He always thought that I was a kid, careless and reckless.

After aunty (Vishal's Mom) came back, I went to meet her. I don't know if she found me good or not but she did say, "You remind me of my elder daughter. When she used to stay at home, this place never used to be silent. Though I really loved this Maggi you made for me, I will really appreciate if you improve your culinary skills. In a matter of five years, you'll be married off and every girl should know the basics of home-making. Vishal told me you are into fashion designing. Some day I would love to wear a saree designed by you."

I think by then aunty had guessed the relation we both shared. Vishal never talked on such matters to his Mom In fact, they hardly conversed, but parents do have a lot of experience and they can understand things better way than we can ever do. That was the first and last time I visited his home.

But just like spring comes to bring joy into our lives, autumn does come back again. The cycle keeps on moving and that is what happened. After Vishal's entry in my life, my life had become a party but it was finally time to face the realities of life. We were nearing our graduation and everyone was busy preparing for their future. Some were engrossed in preparation of CAT, admissions to better universities, placements and what not and it was one of those days, when Vishal had a serious discussion with me regarding this. He had been very quiet since the past few days and I had finally confronted him at his unusual behaviour. I stood with my hands folded, leaning on his bike and waiting for an explanation from him.

"Priyanka, you know I haven't done a single good thing in my life in the past three years, except proposing to you. But now, it's time to prove myself. I promised a good life to you and if I don't work now, I'll never be able to make you mine. I want to achieve something." He did have a point.

"So?"

"So the point is we'll have to stop these daily hangouts and dates. I have been researching for quite some time and I will be joining a good coaching institute after two days for getting selected in Indian Civil Services. I won't be able to meet you daily or pick you up from home. In fact, we might not be able to talk at night even. Will you be able to manage like this?" he asked looking at me with a serious expression on his face.

"Of course, I will be able to. I'll do anything for you. It will be tough in the beginning but I will do. After all, you are doing this for us and I'll be there to support you at every step. I don't want to be a hindrance in your achievements. I love you, baby," I said, hugging him. In the past one month I had begun feeling that Vishal would definitely be with me forever and I had somewhere started accepting him as my man. My doubts of a successful love relation were almost cleared and I felt lucky to know that he was working hard for my sake.

We had a big date before Vishal joined his coaching for I knew times like these would be less in number now. It was my testing time and difficult to spend the day without his company but I kept consoling myself by thinking about his endeavours. I didn't even like spending much time with Vishakha. I normally sat alone or in my work-station, keeping myself engrossed in my fabrics. He did try to talk for 30-40 minutes at night, but dozed off in the middle of our talks. Apart from that, I stared at our pics together and Facebook which became a good distraction for me. All day I used to be active, chatting with anyone, whether I knew that person or not. There was a time I didn't add strangers but now I had begun to. I had no other way out to ward off my loneliness. And it was a good way to chat with strangers for they would never ask you about your past or question you about your present. They will just be happy knowing about you. Half the boys at any social networking site do nothing than flirt around but in the process, you sometimes hit onto some really good people whom you cherish all your life.

"Vishal, it's been a fortnight since we met. I am not going to take much of your time. Just want to have a look at you. If you think your time will be wasted, I'll come around at your coaching or your home, wherever you say," I said, getting restless.

"That is not the point, Priyanka. I am too busy with work and a meeting is totally impossible. Plus if I meet you, I'll get distracted and the whole labour of the week shall go waste if I do not revise on Sunday," he said, citing out his reasons.

"I really want to meet you. Don't you miss me?" I asked, feeling sad about it.

"Of course I do, I love you baby and dumbo is doing all this for you. C'mon, now give me a kiss before you go to sleep," he said lovingly and I fell for his words again.

Things never went straight. We argued more now over silly things and genuine reasons. All we needed was a spark and it didn't take long to have a burning argument over trivial matters.

"You actually don't care. We stay in the same city and we haven't met since the past one month," I roared many a times.

"I have been busy, you know that," he replied.

"Do you think I am a fool? Don't we all study? How much time are you giving to your preparation that you don't even have an hour's time for me? You are up to something that you are hiding from, reasons still unknown to me," I said, getting suspicious.

"So you think I am having an affair?"

"Yes, that could be the reason. You never know. You may have got bored of me and that is why you must have found a new girl for yourself."

"Look, Priyanka, you just can't put unreasonable allegations on me," said Vishal.

"This is something obvious. You are doing something else and you aren't speaking out frankly to me. So, in case I am blaming you for something, it is absolutely genuine. It's your mistake, not mine," my anger spoke, taking over my love for him.

"Stop your nonsense and go to sleep," he hung up the call, before I could react.

I cried, till sleep. Soft sobs turned to wailings but he didn't call back. My pillow remained my sole companion in my moments of suffering. Before sleeping, I sent him a message saying that I loved him but he didn't reply back.

My cell rang at eight in the morning. It said Vishal calling. "Good morning drama queen. Get up, it's already late," he said in a lovely tone.

"What better way to start my day with your morning wish. Morning baby, I love you and I am sorry for last night."

"That's okay. Now get ready for college. My coaching is going to begin, talk to you later. Bye!"

For some days I avoided discussing much about our relation. We conversed on general topics. It was something like we were just communicating, not talking. The connection between us was missing. For me, our friendship had always been a priority but during that period, circumstances had changed. We frequently exchanged dialogues and when we did, it was more of a formality, an effort made to work out our relation.

"Why are you so dull, darling?" Vishakha asked me.

"I just don't feel good Vish. Life has become so boring. I am happy with my work but my personal life is so down the gutters. He doesn't even have time to talk to me *yaar.*"

"Chill, all men are like this. If you want we can search for a better boyfriend for you."

"Shut up, Vish. I just don't understand his behaviour these days. He is busy with his coaching all day and doesn't even talk to me properly. Have you had a talk with him recently?"

"No. He doesn't respond to my messages. I did call him once but he didn't pick and that was when I decided I won't call him again till he calls back. Vish doesn't call boys; boys come after Vish. And whosoever shows attitude doesn't fucking deserve my friendship."

"How time passes by? There was a time when all three of us were together all day and now everyone has gone his or her own way, splitting up the path."

"Happens. We need to face reality. So what, if he isn't giving you time? We can always go for shopping and catch up on some gossip."

"Yes we can, but seriously, I don't feel like going now."

"No excuses, we are going now," Vish said authoritatively.

"I really don't want to. We'll go later."

"Stop being so lousy, lazybumps. Get up, we are going out," she kicked me out from bed and we were soon on our way to give time to our friendship that had taken a backseat from the past month."

And then one day I thought that instead of brooding over the fact that we cannot meet, why not go and give him a surprise? I checked my watch; it was 2 p.m. His coaching would get over by 4 p.m. I had enough time to get ready and reach his coaching. I got dressed with care. I chose a white skirt and a red flared top that he had gifted me. My white ballerinas looked perfect with my attire and I let my hair loose for I knew he loved them like that. A little bit of kohl and my very own Calvin Klein fragrance made it perfect. I reached my destination past before time.

I saw the batch leave but didn't find him. I kept on looking but didn't get a sight of Dumbo. I wondered as to where he had vanished. Thinking that I had lost him, I called him up. He picked up the phone after some time.

"Vishal, where are you?"

"Err...just got over with coaching."

"I am standing at the entrance of your coaching, but can't find you."

"What?" he blurted out as if I had given him a shock.

"Yes. I thought I should give you a surprise but couldn't find you in the crowd."

"Where are you? What was the need to come down here? Ummm...do one thing. Just stay there. I'll see you in a minute."

"Is everything fine, Vishal? You don't seem to be happy about it," I asked questioningly.

"Yes, of course. I was just not expecting. I am at the Xerox shop; will see you in a minute."

I waited for around fifteen minutes. The photocopy shop was at ten step distance but I couldn't find him anywhere. But then I reasoned that he might have gone to some other shop and you often tend to get late at such a place with so many students around to get Xerox copies.

"Hey!" Vishal greeted me with a warm hug.

"Hi!" I said with a smile.

"So, didn't you like the surprise? I thought you'd love having your girlfriend at your step."

"No..no. I loved it."

"Got your notes photocopied?" I asked as I couldn't see anything in his hand. He didn't even have his bag.

"Yeah."

"Let me also see what you guys study at coaching. Where is your bag, Vishal? Do you come emptyhanded over here?" I said, smiling at him, not wanting to sound offensive and suspicious.

"Err...of course not. I do bring my notebook but umm... ummm... Rahul wanted my notes and that is why we went to the photocopy shop but unfortunately the shopkeeper's machine broke down midway so I gave him my register to study for a day."

"Hmmm...my boy is working quite hard these days. Shall we go out somewhere or you have to go home and study?" I asked.

"I have to study but we can spend an hour together."

We went to a coffee shop and as usual, there was no connection in our talks. He didn't even once compliment me which he normally used to do. We didn't leave any topic, friends, news, sports, movies, music, everything but that spark was missing. Nevertheless, I was happy that we finally could sit together and gave time to our relation, away from our busy schedule. I wasn't too happy after the date but I felt better and content as well.

My life moved further. Slowly and gradually, I became used to my daily routine and all I did the whole day was giving my 100 per cent to my love of fabrics and to social networking. I uploaded pics, latest updates of my store and what not. Farmville, City ville became my timepass every day. And then one day as I logged in to my Facebook account, I received a friend request from a guy named Shashank Mittal. No mutual friend, just another flirt I assumed but he had a name that haunted me till date. Something that took me to my past, my fucked up past, the murderer of my castle of dreams with a similar name. *Shashank Agrawal.* But I had to get over all this. I always run away from my past so let me just have a talk with this guy. I need to challenge myself, to know my guts. Why does my past make me go numb? This guy is going to be fun. I instantly made up my mind to talk to him some day. I need to do a research on people with this name, I thought and got back to working on a design.

It was around six in the evening when I received a call from Vishal. It was quite unusual to receive a call from him at this hour. Earlier there was no fix time for us, but now things had changed. His call at any time of the day would sound peculiar now. Anyway I picked up the call.

"Listen Priyanka, Mom has come to know about us through a distant cousin of mine. She saw us the last time we met and since then she has been gathering info about it. So in case you get a call from anybody asking about me or our relationship, just tell her that we are good friends since school, that is okay. There's is no need to talk and discuss much. Hope you are getting me."

"Hmm...Okay. You don't worry, I'll handle things. Take care of yourself," I said getting concerned about him.

"Yes, I will and you too. I don't want any irrelevant person to bother me at this crucial time."

Amazingly, he was more bothered about himself than me. At least that is what I felt but I ignored it again.

Within twelve hours I received a call from an unknown number. Even though Vishal had warned me about the call, I had never expected someone would call me at 3 a.m. to discuss this matter. In fact before picking it up, I was pretty sure it would be some hosteller from my college. But to my surprise, this was an unknown female voice who, without any greeting, straightaway bombarded questions at me. "So Priyanka, what kind of a relation do you exactly share with Vishal?"

A stranger asked a sleepy girl with too much of energy, attitude and anger. As if I would spare her for running my sleep. "Excuse me Ma'am, but I hope you realise that this is no time to call up a person without stating any apology or greeting. I'll answer all your queries but not now. I expect you to take an appointment from me if you really need to talk things out. I am busy right now, okay?" I answered softly and could sense a pang of irritation in her. Man, it's not easy to show an attitude and get away with it.

"Look Priyanka, I want the answer now."

“And Ms. whosoever you are, I am busy with sleep. You can call me up any time in the day and I shall be there to chat with you, okay?”

“Hmm...okay. Then let me know when you are free tomorrow? I'll call you up,” she replied in a tone of loss.

“Okay. Call me up some time in the morning at 7 a.m. I go for a walk then and that's the only time I am free,” I replied in double the attitude she had talked to me with.

Even though the call got disconnected in a fraction of seconds, the hangover remained all night. I couldn't sleep no matter how hard I tried. For once, I thought I should call up Vishal and talk but something within me stopped. By now I was almost clear that she was no cousin; she was something more. She was someone who was trying to take my place, or maybe she had already taken my place. Life is so unpredictable at times. When you feel you have finally figured it out, it has to give you a punch right on your face. I had finally begun to move on with Dumbo when things had changed. It felt crap to talk to a girl who tried to show her proscimily my guy in quite a visible manner. I mean she made me feel like a loser and it was like what the hell was I doing in between them? Though actually the case should have been reverse, but that is how it sounded. I knew that I was heading towards my second breakup. I didn't want to have any conversation with Vishal till the next morning at least. I slept in the morning but woke up at 7 a.m. I saw there were 20 missed calls from Vishal and I was in no mood to talk to him or call him back.

I brushed my teeth and straightaway went to the park with Buster. Within five minutes, I received a call from my ex's present girlfriend. Yes, I had decided I would not compromise on this with Vishal, come what may.

"So Priyanka, hope you are free now?" the mystery woman asked me.

"Yes. Before we begin the bitchy chat, may I know how should I address you?"

"Prachi."

"Okay Prachi, proceed," I replied in an affirmative tone.

"I just wanted to know as to what kind of a relationship do you people share?"

"We are just friends," I said. I don't know why I said this.

"Just friends?" she questioned again.

"Yes, we are friends since school days."

"Thank God," she heaved a sigh of relief.

"I am not done Prachi. I accept Vishal and I are friends since school days. We are best buddies but apart from being my bestie, he is also my boyfriend since the past year and being his girlfriend, I have the right to ask you that why you are so interested in our relationship."

"What? Did you just say you are his girlfriend? I am his girlfriend since the last two months."

"Wow! That means he has been double crossing us. Anyway, tell him that he is a big asshole and he has just lost his one girlfriend," I blurted out in anger.

"Hold on! Priyanka, I wanted to ask you few things as well."

"Sure, go ahead."

"Did you guys in any way get..ummm...physical or something like that?"she asked me.

I wonder what's up with girls these days. She still wanted to inquire about such a thing. I mean, if I would have come to know that my guy was doing such a thing, I would leave him then and there. In fact I exactly did that a few minutes earlier.

"Huh! No way. I would never do such a thing with him. He did want to, but I never gave in because I know men are bastards. And in case you want to inquire about kissing then 'yes' we kissed. We roamed about the whole of Delhi NCR and we went to Manali too. Anything else you want to know?"

"Nope. Thanks Priyanka."

"Prachi, what course are you doing presently?" I asked out of curiosity. I almost thought she was an intern (as she sounded too young to be a doctor) in a mental hospital and had lost her brain while treating all the insane people out there.

"I just got promoted to Class XII. Why?"

I tell you man, I was drinking buttermilk then and all of it dropped out of my mouth when I heard she was younger to me. I felt like laughing at the loser guy and pitied this girl.

"Nothing, just asked. Anyway, all the best for your life with Vishal."

"Thanks, Priyanka. I hope you two are over now and I get him as my boyfriend. You know, he followed me for a span of two months, so that I would talk to him once."

"Oh! Is it? Great Prachi. You guys are truly meant for each other. I have some work now. I should hang up the call now. Bye Prachi."

What had happened to my life? I flopped on the bench in the park, trying to digest the things. Was this a hoax call or a genuine one? I had finally moved on in life. The presence of Vishal had started becoming blurred with the passage of time, but there was a hope that he was with me, an empty one though. Sadly, we always cling to hope. I had just had a semi breakup. I had to officially call it off with Vishal. Things weren't straight between us since quite some time and I knew they would never be now.

I felt a different kind of emptiness within me and I filled it with vodka. Scenes from the past came racing up my mind, so all I could do was run to the bar to have a drink. I knew I had to go back home, so I just kept it to two pegs. When I returned, Mom and Dad said that they were going out for dinner and expected me to join them. I declined, saying I was tired. Yes, I was tired and sick, not physically but mentally. I plugged in my earphones, Lady Gaga gave me company for quite some time and I soon fell asleep.

My cell phone had been ringing all day, but I did not pick up any call. Every call that came was from Vishal, but I kept on working. At four in the evening, when I finally reached out for my cell, I saw 100 missed calls all were from Vishal. There were quite a number of messages as well. I read the last one that asked me to reach Costa Coffee at 4:30 p.m. I didn't want to go but from inside I wanted to see his face for one last time. My insides were burning. I was feeling helpless. I was a loser to fall for a guy again. It felt too bad to get dumped the second time. I somehow found my car keys and left alone. I didn't want the driver to take me anywhere. I wanted my own isolation. I drove like mad unaware of the traffic rules. I wonder why no one stopped me. Was the Delhi traffic police sleeping that time?

It had begun to rain heavily and it was getting difficult to drive but I kept on going. And then finally came a point when I could not drive further. I parked the car and got down. It didn't even take two minutes to get drenched in the rain. I kept on walking, unaware of my surroundings, totally unknown to my destination. I don't know for how long I walked but I remember waking up from my thoughts when a truck stopped right in front of me and Vishal came to fetch me.

I looked into his eyes. Everyone said he had killer eyes. He surely was a killer. He had killed me from inside. As I looked at him, all the past year's moments flashed before my eyes. It was truly impossible to believe that I had again been dumped and that too by my best friend. The promises he had made to me were fake, the times he had spent with me were all bogus, everything was just plain pretence. Or was he truly genuine then, but had got over me by now? But isn't true love meant to be forever? He had said he truly loved me and I had become so dependent on him that life would really be nothing without him. I really didn't know where things were going wrong.

We stood outside Costa Coffee. He asked me to come in but I refused. "I don't want to waste time in having coffee and I am happy to take in all the news you have for me in the rain. I am not going in, at least with you."

"Priyanka, you have to face it. You and I are over. I am dating Prachi now."

"Yes, I know," I said, nodding my head. I had a mixture of feelings. I wanted to stop him and slap him at the same time.

"We have been in a relation since two months and..."

"And you have been double crossing me. Why Vishal, why? Where had I gone wrong? Can't we just start all of it again with a fresh new beginning?" I asked, cutting him midway.

"No Priyanka, that's really not possible."

"Are you sure?" I asked.

"Yes and you have to promise me one thing," he said.

I thought he would ask me to stay strong and all that shit but he said something else and because of which he did have to face a few consequences.

"You'll do no harm to Prachi. You tend to be too aggressive in your ways often and I just want to request you to not try and break this relation."

Slap! Slap! Slap! Yes, that is what I gave him in return. "Shut up, you fucking bastard. It's my life and I'll do things my way, got it. You are no one to tell me what is wrong and what is right. What do you guys think of yourself? You can play with girls anytime you wish and throw them off from your life when you get bored? Now, just wait and watch what happens to your love for Prachi," I threatened and darted off.

I didn't want to stay further with him. I had had enough of this love breakup drama. I won't let myself suffer any more. The rain hadn't stopped and pools of water had already formed on the roads. I walked till the parking lot and had no more strength to drive back home. Unknowingly my driver spotted me. He was off duty but insisted on dropping me home.

Alas! Vishal was in love again but not with me.

TIME TO HIT BACK

My cell rang, waking me up from my thoughts of the past. It was Vishakha telling me to be ready at six in the evening. She would be coming to pick me as she wanted me to stay at her house for the night. I didn't want to go but I accepted as even I wanted to be away from all the stupid thoughts running across my mind. It is amazing how all such moments make an impact on us. Once they come into our thoughts, they don't leave till the end. I had been lost in sad thoughts since the past one hour and hadn't realised. I had been sitting all alone at the Metro station, thinking about all the shit that had happened in my life. Why did it happen to me? What was my fault? Was haste bringing me this in return?

I was walking back home when I received a message from Shashank on Facebook. Oh! It was not my Shashank; it was the Facebook Shashank. Shashank Mittal who had recently been added to my friend list and somehow we used to talk a lot.

"Hey! How are you? How was the day?" He asked.

"It went fine. How was yours?" He asked.

"Like always, crap happens in my life. I am telling you Ritika is screwing up my life," his daily ritual of cribbing about his girlfriend

began. I couldn't blame him either; long distance relations are surely a pain in the neck.

"What happened today?"

"Nothing new, she doesn't want to talk to me. Whenever I call her, she is busy or has to study. As it is, she has given me 9 p.m to 10 p.m. to call her up and even in that period, she hardly talks for ten minutes. I don't know why I called her up at a different time today, thinking that being a weekend she would talk to me. But she picked up my call only to say that she was busy studying and didn't want to get disturbed."

Boy, didn't this guy understand that this girl was not interested in him. She was just playing around. Why was he behaving like this? But then every time I thought of him, I saw my past in him. When Shashank had started ignoring me, I used to restlessly wait for him.

"Don't worry, she'll be fine. When you know she is a studious kind of a person, why do you call her at other hours of the day?"

God, I wasn't making any sense but I had to make him feel better. I didn't know I had become a social worker when it came to emotions.

"Yeah, my mistake. I'll take care of it next time," he signed off, saying so.

Shashank Mittal had become a good friend in my Facebook list and we used to talk daily. He had a girlfriend of one year. Ritika, who studied at Manipal while he studied at College of Engineering, Pune. I wonder how they maintained such a longdistance relationship. I mean today people in the same city weren't able to handle a healthy relation, so keeping a long distance relationship was out of the way. Amazingly, they had met in one of those Kota coaching centres and he had been mesmerised by her since Day one. According to him, it was love at first sight, but I had no belief in such kind of love. But he was a friend, I had to stay by his side and moreover, I could sense that he did love that bitch sincerely. May be love at first sight is possible. I had heard his love story number of times and he never seemed to get tired of narrating it again and again.

He had told me how he used to touch her curly hair when she sat in front of him in the class or how he would run across the building just to have a look at her. I had almost etched the scene in my mind when he had narrated his story of proposing to her. In fact even I loved hearing his stories for as you all know, I am a diehard romantic, sorry I was a diehard romantic but I still loved interacting with people who were in love or had a true love by their side.

I came back home, packed my bags and got ready. I knew Vishakha would be reaching at six sharp. In no time, I was at Vish's place. It felt good to be in her room after a long time. It was going to be fun, I knew.

Vish's Mom had prepared her famous chilly chicken and I could in no way resist it. It was at her place only that I had learnt to eat non vegetarian. My family was strictly vegetarian, but Dad used to have it during official meetings. And later even I began to eat though my Mom had no other option than to prepare it for two crazy people of the house.

"So tell me the story," Vish said, while we were eating.

"Food first," I said, giggling.

She gave me a 'no one can help you' look again.

Anyway I did sit down to narrate the story of Prachi and Vishal. Vishakha had been a great friend to Vishal but somehow distance had arisen in their friendship and now they weren't in touch even.

"So what are you planning to do now?" she asked.

"Nothing, absolutely nothing! Actually I don't know if I should really do something rather than brooding over it," I replied.

"C'mon, you should do something, something wicked, something that would make him guilty or at least irritate him."

"How?" I asked as I was really clueless.

"The usual. Return his gifts but not to him. Send them to Prachi," she said, with her eyes full of mischief.

"Are you crazy? Why should I part with my teddy?" I said sulkily.

"I'll get one for you, idiot. You will just brood over things if you get to see them daily."

"Okay, done."

I was excited to take my revenge. Somehow it didn't feel any more that I had just had a break-up. I felt good that I had been freed of a moron. And thank God, I wasn't with a loser like him. We had some Chicken Ceaser Salad and simultaneously began to search for Prachi on Facebook. Awesome discovery. Prachi was a student of our school. 'She is gone for sure,' we gave a high five to each other. In no time my very own detective Vishakha had found out that Prachi was a Science student, who was a little dumb but over smart. I could sense that after I come to know that to she had got committed to Vishal. She already had five slaves to her credit and whom she didn't refer to as her ex-boyfriends. Okay, so Vishal was going to be the sixth one. Boy! This was going to be fun. She stayed at some PG now as she was taking some serious coaching for medical. I could visualise her seriousness towards her goal. I knew these kind of girls either got what they wanted or lost to the most unexpected point.

"Vish, I was thinking that I should have done the same with Shashank too. It would have served him right," I said sarcastically.

"I thought you loved him."

"I love nobody."

"So, what do you plan to do now?"

"Nothing, I just want to enjoy life," I replied.

"Oh yes! Who have you been replying to the whole day? Your cell phone keeps on buzzing every fifteen minutes," Vishaka pointed out.

"Oh! It's Shashank, Shashank Mittal. I told you about that Facebook guy. We keep on chatting all day, all thanks to Facebook messages."

The next day when I reached home, the first thing I did was to gather all the gifts Vishal had given me.

- The pink teddy bear given on my birthday.

- The brown teddy with a heart saying, "I Love You."
- The blue coloured BFF coffee mug.
- The photo frame with the three of us in it.
- The personalised Happy Birthday Coffee mug.
- The pink pen stand with 'I love writing poetry' scribbled in red over it. I always wondered why he insisted on writing poems when I knew I was a mess at it.
- 5-6 key rings. I didn't want to, but had to.
- I opened my wardrobe and picked out each and every apparel that he had gifted me. There were around eight but revenge was making me go red with rage.
- A few cards and curions and I was done.

After collecting them, I needed a small carton and if you are thinking I am just going to put them and send to Prachi's address, you are wrong. I took a knife and cut half slit the pink teddy's throat, poured some red paint on its neck, inserted a few pins and needles in the brown teddy's tummy, smashed all his mugs, and pen stand, tore his cards and cut every outfit he had given. As for the key rings, they were spared and a note was inserted.

This one is for your guy.

Thanks for all the love he gave me. This is my hate for you.

Priyanka

The only thing that was left was wrapping up the box with red coloured paper. With the help of Vishakha, we managed to take it to the courier office. Though I had to pay a hefty amount for such a heavy package, I didn't care at all. Vish had already got Prachi's address and we laughed off the incident. It was time to celebrate. I gave a formal break up party to my friends at Bistro cum Spaghetti Chicken, at Select City Walk. It was real fun. Later we headed to 'The Coffee Bean and Tea Leaf' for some awesome blossom coffee and desserts. The warm chocolate cake was terribly yummy. It was time to enjoy and celebrate life.

SPICY AND TASTY LIFE

I wanted to turn nasty, like really nasty. Every day I worked my asses off at my workstation but evenings were fun with my girlie gang and time spent on commenting on guy. Oh! God, it was real fun. Vish always tried to pick out men for me but when I had a talk with them, I just felt like banging his head on the wall. In a span of ten days I had gone dating with five men and found none of them close to my style. I wondered when would Vish grow up in her taste for men as they were generally her friends or would be boyfriends.

DATE # 1

Vish had made me wear a black one piece with black stilettos that made it really difficult for me to walk. She had given my eyes the smoky look with a nude coloured lipstick. Small black dangles with my hair left loose looked good on me. My latest black clutch from Miss Bennett looked super cool with the combination. When I first saw him entering the place, I thought he was a father of two, coming to have fun with his family. Unfortunately he came up to me asking my name and introducing himself as 'Rishabh Bajaj.' I was already going mad after taking a look at him and his name made me go back to the days of one of the K daily soap by Ekta Kapoor. Why were all Rishabh Bajaj oldies? I almost thought I was talking to the wrong man but I checked out his pic in my cell phone and it really was him. How stupid of me to not have a look at his picture before.

"So you a designer, right?"

"Yes."

"See if we begin to date, you can be the designer for my company. Won't it be great?"

Was he here to date me or have a business deal in which he could get a fashion designer for free?

I just smiled back, trying to speak as little as possible. He gave out the menu card to me but amazingly gave the order himself before I could utter a word.

"You know this chicken is my favourite. I have been coming here for five years and they have never failed in their services. By the way, what's your full name Ms. Priyanka?"

He didn't even know my full name and had come to date me.

"Priyanka Bajaj," I replied smiling. From inside I felt like tying him up with a rope and shooting him continuously for ten minutes nonstop.

"Oh! Wow, that's really great. It increases our chances of getting married," he said and started roaring.

He laughed as if he wanted the whole of the restaurant to hear him out and smiled shyly in the end. I felt like saying, "Who the hell would date you, moron? Forget about marriage."

I finished off with the dinner as soon as I could and almost ran across the road for a taxi. I didn't want him to leave me in his car. I couldn't tolerate him any longer.

DATE # 2

Tarun Sabarwal, my next date. A typical Punjabi guy with the typical accent and ways. Period. Even before going out with him, I knew he would be handsome but his brains were expected to be lost. And I was so right. He came in his Audi to pick me up. He had great body and his dressing sense was really cool, spiked hair, black from top to bottom and musky fragrance that surrounded us in the car. He took me to the one of the best restaurants of Defence Colony but when he opened his mouth it had to be stupid always. And man, I had a really hard time making him utter my name.

"Princa, what would you like to have?" he asked, showing his extra sparkling white teeth.

"Whatever you like, Tarun. And my name is Priyanka, not Princa," I corrected him.

"Yeah..yeah..that's what I am saying, Princa."

I knew that very instant it was futile to correct him any more."Tarun, you can call me Pia. That would be better."

"Sure Princa, I mean Pia."

I am telling you this was really a great relief.

He ordered a lot of chicken and ate it all. When the food came in front of me, I felt as if it was for at least ten people but it was just for two of us and he had it all. I wondered if he had come to actually date me or suffice his hunger needs. I thought he hadn't eaten for five days but he surprised me by saying that he had had tandoori chicken for snacks. God, I would never be able to survive with him. I really pitied his future wife. She would die preparing food for him.

I really don't know why I had worn a deepneck kurta that day. He had tried 'n' number of times to peek a boo at my cleavage. Unfortunately, he wasn't successful. Need I say that he wasn't fit for me?

DATE # 3

He was finally dating a student like me. But he was one geek I had ever met with black spectacles and closed collar buttons, he looked the usual geeky guy. In just half an hour, he had updated my knowledge on technology. He was to go to Microsoft for student exchange program in two months and man, he really deserved that position.

I don't know what had made me take him to a bookstore. I had to get some Mills and Boons to read and he gifted me some techno loaded magazines and books. I didn't know what I would do with them. Thank God, I had a gadget freak brother. I planned to gift them to him. He carried the heavy books all the way and when we came to the parking, he disclosed me something that blew my brains off.

"Priyanka, I don't know how you would find it but I can't drive on this crowded road. Should we take a bus from here?"

I took the keys from him, wore my helmet and made him sit behind me. I drove his Activa all the way to Mandi House. There is a meals on wheels kind of Chinese food joint there and I have always loved having noodles there. We ordered some momos, noodles and chicken manchurian. I fed the cat whom I met daily there, sitting under the car. It is damn cute, I must tell you. While I fed her, Dipanshu kept on jumping from place to place as he was scared of the cat. And oh! Did I tell you this geeky guy's name was

Dipanshu? He was different but possessed a special cuteness. Before seeing him off, I pulled his cheeks and he gave me a small packet of sugar coated candies, smiling shyly at me. He was really very adorable.

DATE # 4

The next in line was a tall guy who had a trademark smile on his face all day long. He came in formals to meet me. I wondered if he had office on weekends or was he to attend one after our date? I came to know he was into marketing and I understood the reason for his smile and attire.

"Priyanka, I think we should have coffee at this newly opened cafe in Vasant Kunj. It is really good. They are my client and they will even offer you discount for your next two visits as well. I think if you come around with me, you will really like it and then you can always come around with your friends or with me again."

Business here again. Why are men so obsessed with business? I mean I know they were his clients but that surely didn't mean he had to take me there. Marketing here too. When will boys learn to maintain a balance between their professional life and personal life? We did go to the coffee house he had suggested and he was actually right. The place was good from ambience to taste, everything was perfect. But his marketing skills had been infused so deeply in his blood that his normal conversation also sounded like marketing to me. "You should try out this brand; it is really helpful. You know they are my client and I'll even get you discounts from them."

God, I was so pissed off with this habit of his that every time he opened his mouth, he'd talk of his clients and discounts. I shut him from my Facebook friend list and stopped replying to his messages. Vishakha felt I shouldn't have done so as discount coupons always helped. I felt like killing her.

DATE # 5

I wouldn't want to call it a date but then this guy was really good at heart. I was in no mood to go out with him but Vishakha had pushed me into it. I hadn't even dressed properly, ice blue jeans with long white top, white ballerinas, white wristwatch and a white hair band topped up with a little kohl and lip gloss was what I had sported for the day. The moment we met, I told him I had allotted this day for shopping but this sudden date had made me drop my plans.

He instantly agreed to give me company in shopping and we all know that taking a girl out for shopping is a real tough job. I took him to Sarojini Nagar and Lajpat Nagar, picking out so much stuff, window shopping and what not. From cheap bangles to *kurtis* and laces, I made him aware of everything girlie that day but I really have to speak about his patience. He never showed a sign of irritation. He kept on helping me out with picking up the bags and he even paid for everything I purchased. In return, I gifted him a shirt for helping me out for the day. We ate *pani puri* and *chole bhature* at the roadside vendors, drank all kinds of juices in between and clicked on very well. Finally, in the evening, we sat at CCD, totally exhausted. He showed me pics of his friends and family and I even got to know about his dream project and past relationships. Abhilash became a real good friend in a short span of time but that was all he could be. Both of us knew we could never gel as a couple and we had our own ambitions to work out on first. But we promised to be in contact with each other through messages and social networking.

With those five dates I was done with boys. I told Vishakha I wouldn't go for blind dates any more and she agreed. I hadn't forgotten to mention that her taste in men was really bad. The eleventh day, when I was sitting with Vishakha in my workshop, Vishal entered. I was shocked to see him, at least after what I had done to him.

"Why are you doing this, Priyanka?" he asked.

"I am done with whatever I had to do. Just go away from my way, okay," I replied with a stern look on my face.

"I hope you wouldn't do anything like this again," he told me. Was he trying to challenge me?

"I had thought I wouldn't do anything now but you seem to challenge my guts, Vishal," I answered haughtily.

"I am not challenging you. I just want you not to create problems for us," he said softly to me. I felt pity for him.

"Us? Eh? Cool, you and Prachi. Well, let me tell you if I was in your place, I would have never done such a stupid act after knowing her history. In any case, it's your life, your girl and I know you aren't serious about love. Go away from here, Vishal or I would punch you really hard this time. I pity you today, and I am thankful that you don't have your Dad around because had he seen his son in this state, he would have never been able to bear it." I said this to him and the moment I had uttered this, he froze for a minute and left without saying a word more.

After he was gone, Vishakha patted my back for the super awesome reply I had given him. Sometimes a bitter reply is what is needed to stop one from blabbering, and that is what I did. I don't know why but I felt like taking my revenge against Shashank too, but then I stopped. Matters of past shouldn't matter me anymore.

❖ ❖ ❖

Vishal says :

Everyone thinks I am a bad guy. Yes I am the bad guy. I left her for someone else but does everyone know why I left her? No, no one knows because if I tell you, you guys will laugh at me and say you just need an excuse to get a new girl. I know it has been a case of infidelity on my part but do you guys think I could have possibly provided the luxuries to Priyanka that she is surrounded by now? No, never. My Dad was a wealthy doctor and he left a lot for his wife and children but I am a spoilt child of the dead doctor. I have messed up my career. Even if I get myself a decent job after my Masters, I would never be able to compete with her Dad. No way can I do this.

I was in a dilemma regarding this for long and then Prachi came into my life. I knew she was the girl who would help me divert my mind. I began following her, imbibed the playboy ways and took her as my girlfriend. It isn't that I was totally right. I had started liking Prachi. It was fun to flirt again. With Priyanka, I had gone far in time span only but in the relationship,everything was getting boring. We hadn't gone further than a kiss. It was not that I was desperate but I had waited for long. Though the last time we met it felt that she had actually begun to love me but there was no use carrying forward the relation. I had grown over her.

She would never admit but there were tear stains on the note and the box. I knew she had cried. She would never tell this to anyone. This is what I hate about her. She will hide her emotions from everyone, trying to present herself as the strongest and the coolest. From within even she knows she is a soft little girl. Our journey together was till this destination only. I hope she will make a wiser decision in future, considering the fact how crazy she is. The Dumbo-Drama queen union ends here.

A NEW BEGINNING

"I think you should give her a surprise by going to her place," I suggested to Shashank Mittal as a new way to woo his girlfriend.

"Are you crazy? MANIPAL is 1,000 kms away from my place and I am sure she wouldn't meet me there. She will have to tell her friends about me and that would mean maligning her image. Wonder what she means by this."

"Does she really love you?" I asked him, getting irritated.

"I don't know but I do love her for sure."

"Are you crazy, Shashank? How can you be so crazy about a girl? She ignores you all day long. She has time for her studies and her friends but not you. She can talk hours to her sisters but not you," I told him angrily on Facebook.

In my hearts of heart I knew there was something fishy about this girl. She wouldn't be talking to her sisters for hours; it had to be someone else. But when would this blind guy realise this?

" Did you wish Shashank yesterday?" he asked. Yes I had told him about Shashank though it was a concocted story.

"No."

"Why?"

"What is the need to? I don't want to bring out the dead from the coffin."

"I think you should have waited for him, Priyanka," he said, for he didn't know the real story. I could have waited if he had waited for me.

So you must be wondering as to what I had told the new Shashank about my old Shashank. Well, I cooked up a story. On asking me whether I had a boyfriend or not, I had told him that I was single, but had one earlier. He had cajoled me into telling my love story. So I had said that I loved a guy named Shashank and even he loved me back but was selected in NDA after school. He didn't want me to suffer in a long distance relationship considering the discipline one has to maintain in the Army. So he freed me from all bonds. The new Shashank felt I should have waited for him but how could I tell him that love was never in my destiny? I could never get the man I love because for every man felt I was just a case of infatuation.

We had been talking regularly for six months now and he had become a great friend. I loved talking to him. I had become a Love Guru for him but with time I had begun to see a few changes in him. He had finally begun to accept Ritika for what she was and she wouldn't change.

"Why don't you leave Ritika?" I asked one day.

"I won't ever do such a crime. Breaking up is like getting torn into two pieces and I would never do such a ghastly thing," he responded. I somehow liked his reply.

In the meanwhile I put my detectives into action. I had cleverly gathered all the necessary info on Ritika so that it would be easy to locate her. I passed on the same to Vishakha who had spread the word in her extra large group of friends and from one of the sources we came to know that Ritika was having an affair with her classmate at Manipal. She had been double crossing him, bloody bitch. I felt sad for Shashank and planned to somehow know about the guy with whom she was having the affair.

Since the day I had come to know the truth about Ritika, I had been feeling too bad for him but I couldn't muster the courage to tell him the truth, lest he broke off our friendship. Every day I thought of a way to tell him about her, but lost all the strength when it came to putting it all in words. In between I had collected all information about Ritika's classmate Azhar with whom she was having an affair. Surprisingly he happened to be Vishakha's friends schoolmate and it became easier for us to track him down.

"Hey, may I ask you something," Shashank asked me on Facebook the other day.

"Yeah...sure."

"Can we exchange phone numbers? I know it's a little creepy to ask for such a thing especially when we chat almost all day long on Facebook, but it's like that when messages don't reach on time through FB or my net pack ends or I am out, it feels empty to not be able to chat with you. Plus, it would be nice to talk to you on the phone. I have always wondered what your voice would be like."

I was a little amazed at his sudden request for my cell number even though this wasn't something new for me. Many people had asked me for my contact number and with a few I had exchanged numbers as well. But his 'it feels empty without our chats' made me wonder if he had started liking me! No way, he already loved his girlfriend too much and I knew we were just friends. But still I wanted to hold onto the friendship and there was always time to exchange phone numbers.

"I understand your sentiments but I am sorry I can't give you my cell number now," I replied.

I got back to my work. Sadly there was a stupid client who just wasn't satisfied with any of my designs. God, if she really wanted something so good , why was she not prepared to spend some more bucks and go to Manish Malhotra for getting the perfection she desired? Why did people want more for less money? Her fiancée was coming over to meet her and she wanted to look striking. And then I finally gorged into that emerald green that Shashank had suggested. During one of our chats, he had said that he always wanted to see Ritika in an emerald green dress, preferably Indian. I thought why not try out something in that colour and lo behold. When I showed this to the idiotic client of mine, she loved it. She loved it so much that she hugged me in front of everyone. I was a little embarrassed but it was okay. I had finally offered what we call 'customer satisfaction.'

"Hey, guess what? You saved me from losing one of my clients," I sent a message to Shashank that evening.

"How did I do that?"

"You remember telling me about the emerald green dress for Ritika? I used the same colour and idea for my client. She loved it. I owe you a treat," I replied happily.

"Oh! Wow... that's great. By the way, what's the name of your store?" he asked.

"Bianca."

"Why did you call it 'Bianca'?"

"Because it sounds chic," I laughed as I typed the stupid reply.

"Really?" he asked with a astonishment.

"Yes."

"So this is the firangi version of Priyanka, right?"

"Nothing like that. Though it sounds similar to my name, maybe that is why I like this name," I answered his query.

"Okay, agreed."

It had been two days since Shashank's birthday had passed, the old Shashank, my ex and I hadn't felt like calling him. But then in the afternoon I received a call. It was the time of the day when I am super sleepy. Since it was from a new number I didn't even think it could be Shashank. If I would have known I would have never picked it up.

"How are you, Priyanka?" a male voice asked me. Instantly I recognised that it was Shashank Agrawal, but I pretended to be unaware of his true identity.

"I am sorry but may I know who am I speaking to?" I replied politely.

"You didn't recognise me?"

I felt like saying, "No, you fat head," but I controlled myself and said, "I am sorry but I can't recall you."

"Well, Shashank here."

"Oh! It's you. We haven't been in touch, so it took me time to identify you," I replied modestly.

"So how are you?" he asked. I don't know why but his voice seemed to crack, at least that is what I thought.

"I am fine. What's up at your end?" I queried.

"Nothing much. I wanted to say something."

"Yes, go on."

"Priyanka, I am sorry. I am sorry for what I did to you. I can only get your hate in return and that is what I deserve. I know I have been cruel to you, but could you please try forgiving me for old times' sake?" he said and I could hear his sobs in between.

I felt a different kind of rage rush down my veins that moment. I even felt like cutting off both the best friends into small pieces and feeding them to Buster. What did they think of me? A doll. Was I a toy for them that whenever they liked they could play and whenever they got bored, they could throw me away? I wasn't going to forgive them. I'd had enough of their nonsense. I wasn't an excess baggage.

"Shashank, where is Nitika?" I asked, trying to control my anger.

"She left me four months back. She felt that I wasn't husband material. She didn't want to stay with a man who smoke and drank. I tried to persuade her, but she went away. I tried to stop myself from drinking but I had already become an addict. I couldn't leave alcohol and so she left me. I couldn't even gather the courage to talk to you all this while. I called up Vishal yesterday to ask for his forgiveness and I came to know that you two have split up. I almost felt as if my roof had crashed down on my head," he said, but I really didn't know what was the need to tell me this long story? I was done with him.

"So, what exactly do you want? You want to play around with me and have fun again? You wish to play with my emotions again. You are one guy who will always be cheap. Your IIT tag is nothing but bullshit for me because you have still not learnt the art of living. This 'sorry' should have come to me at least a year back, but it didn't and I am sorry, but I will never forgive you. You know who I am? A typical Delhi girl with a blabbering tongue but I am not a slut. Every Delhi girl is not a pros just because she dresses sexily and talks frankly. Keep this in mind and never ever try to call me again because if you do, I will throw shit on your bloody damn face." Saying so, I hung up the call. I didn't want to keep any contacts with the two bastards of my life. They were history now and I never ever wanted to unearth the dead from their graves.

I rushed out of my home that very moment, took my scooty and headed for Ice Cube at GIP. I needed to get high. I loved the darkness and the loud music. It helped me drain out the temper in me. I danced and drank; I drank and danced. I took a smoke. It made me feel better. I took another cigarette and I took another one again. I was planning to light my fourth one when Abhilash snatched it from my mouth. I was shocked to see him. His eyes spewed anger. I laughed, looking at him and said, "Hey, surprised to see you here. Let's have a drink together."

"Good girls don't drink," he replied, smiling at me.

"I am not a good girl, I am a bad bad girl," I sang out aloud. I had got a little high by then.

"No, you aren't. Come, let's sit outside."

"Nooooooo... I am a bad, bad girl. I want to drink. I am a bad bad girl..hiccup..hiccup...just one more please," I said.

"Okay, what do you want to have?" he asked.

"I want to have one fried Vishal and one Shashank *masala* with chicken salad. And yes, Blue Lagoon too."

"What? What did you just say?" Abhilash asked looking confused. How could he understand what I meant.

But after that one more hiccup, I lost consciousness. I don't remember what happened then. The only thing I remember was waking up in a car with Abhilash sitting in front in the driver's seat. My head ached like hell.

"How come I am here? And where are we driving to?"

He gave a big smile and said, "So you are finally back to your senses, bad,bad girl?"

I remembered everything then and smiled back at him embarrassingly.

"You know what? I have been driving for an hour with you not knowing where to take you. I couldn't take you back to your place or my place. I was wondering when you would come back to your senses. In fact if you hadn't woken up in the next thirty minutes, I would have called Vishakha. Coffee?" he asked giving his trademark smile.

"Sure," I said.

"You look good. Royal blue suits you."

"Really? I thought royal blue doesn't suit dusky beauties. I had randomly picked this up."

"C'mon, don't you know dusky beauties are the sexiest ones?"

"Yes, I agree."

While we were having coffee, he asked me, "Who is fried Vishal and *masala* Shashank?"

I began to laugh and so did he and I told him everything about my life, beginning from how I had met Shashank to how I threw them out of my life I felt light after sharing my story with him. It felt as if a burden had been lifted off. As I left that day, I knew I had found a good friend in Abhilash. That one date had turned good for me, we were friends and that's all we wanted to be.

AWESOME BLOSSOM

My life had become awesome. The winds never felt so calm and soothing; a feeling of freedom surrounded me. When I woke up in the morning, I thanked God for giving me a day. I had some goals to achieve, great friends like Abhilash, Vishakha and the new Shashank. Shashank Agrawal had finally made his exit from my life. All thanks to the cool technology, blocking numbers was easy. I loved the block feature. Whoever irritated me or I disliked someone, I used the block tab freely. I joined the Art of Living, read their journals regularly and truly loved their style, at least they didn't back slash at youth. They understood our sentiments and moulded us accordingly. YES+ is something every young mind should join. You meet a new you through this programme of theirs. I was and am still the same whacky girl I used to be but a little more experienced in life.

Love is that which you cannot fully express or hide. Beauty is that which you cannot possess or renounce. Truth is that which you cannot avoid.

-Sri Sri Ravi Shankar

In one of my Yes+ sessions, I came across this quote and I was reminded of Shashank. Was I doing the right thing in hiding the truth? Unveiling the truth was so tough for me. What if he didn't accept it? What if he was to break up our friendship? We had a long session on truth and trust that day. I was too confused in this area. I didn't know what had to be done, but I had to decide and take action. And it had to be taken early.

That evening when I returned, I was determined to tell him the truth anyway. I had collected all the info and had my proofs ready in case I needed them.

"Hey, how was the day?" I received a message from him on Facebook.

"Great; how was yours?"

"Hectic is what I would say. How is your Art of Living going on?"

"It's going fine. I think this has been among the good decisions I made in my life."

"I have never thought of getting into these kind of spiritual organisations, but some people do get a lot of mental peace on joining. I wish you all the luck."

"Thanks. How is Ritika?"

"She must be fine. Last night she was good and so shall she be today."

"Hmm...does she care for you?"

"I know she doesn't but I can't let go off this relation."

"Shashank, listen to me. I want to tell you something but you will have to promise me that this will never hinder our friendship. The truth will be hard to digest but you will have to be strong," I wrote to him and it took at least ten minutes to press the Reply tab.

"What do want to say? I will listen patiently without any interference and I promise it won't come in the way of our friendship."

"Shashank, Ritika is cheating on you..."

ERASE

"Shashank, I wanted to say that..."

ERASE

"Ritika has been double crossing you.."

HELL NO, ERASE

"Shashank, Ritika is not the right girl for you."

"Why do you feel so?" he asked.

"That is because she has been trying to cheat on you. She is having an affair with her classmate Azhar. And when she is not talking to you, she is actually jabbering away with him. They spend every moment together at college. She is making a fool out of you. She is a bitch. If you think I am lying, then I want to tell you that I have proof."

I waited for fifteen long minutes but didn't get any reply.

"Shashank, are you there?"

"Yes and I had a feeling that such a kind of thing was happening around. But this can't change things. I can't leave her even if she has been into infidelity. I can't be like her. She has been my first love and I would never dump her like this. The day she wants to leave me, she can."

I was amazed to his reaction. Could a person be so selfless even in today's times? I was awestruck at his response, such a vast difference between two people with the same name. Shashank Agrawal had ruined his life for his own selfish reasons and Shashank Mittal was ready to sacrifice his life for a girl who didn't even care for his feelings. People should learn something from him. That day respect for him grew in my eyes. I learnt the virtue of selflessness and sacrificing your life for love.

I felt lighthearted after telling him the truth and his views on the relationships had already impressed me. When Vish came to my place in the afternoon, I was all gaga over his goodness.

"He is crazy," Vish said.

"No, he is awesome," I defended him.

"What awesome *yaar*? You get easily impressed by guys. He is the biggest stupid in my eyes. I am telling you he will keep dying for this girl and she will never come to him. He is just spoiling his own life. I always thought boys were dogs and he has proved himself."

"How?" I asked, astonished.

"By being faithful to his girl," she said and started giggling. I couldn't control myself from laughing either.

Life went smoothly after that and Abhilash and Vishakha became really good friends. I was noticing some changes in her but I didn't speak, lest she started being the lioness again. I kept mum but observed her proximity to him. She would never spend time with a guy, especially if he wasn't her boy. She wasn't only what she called as wasting her time with him but was also involved in having telephonic conversations with him regularly.

"So what's up!"

As usual, I was chatting away with Shashank.

"Nothing much. I took a decision today," I replied.

"And what was that?" he asked.

"I will quit drinking and smoking."

"That's great news. When did you begin drinking?"

"After Shashank left me."

"And at what frequency do you drink?"

"Whenever I am sad."

"I hope you will not drink anymore."

"Yes I will try to but every time I turn sad, I head towards some Vodka."

"You will never be sad now, I promise."

"Really?" I asked out of curiosity.

"Yes, a friend's promise."

There were a few things that were bringing us closer. It may have been unknown to both of us but situations were changing and they were changing for good. The world suddenly started looking more beautiful.

You make my life colourful.

This was the first message I received from him on my cell phone. I had finally exchanged numbers with him.

Thank you for the compliment.

I didn't know what else I should say. I wish I could say the same to him but refrained myself from doing it.

You once told me you write poetry. I want to read some of them. I had told this to him long time back and amazingly he remembered them.

Yeah. I used to.

Send me one now.

He wanted me to send him those crapy poems.

Now?

He was crazy. My poems were too stupid to be read.

Yes.

But I had to give in to his demands, I knew. He would eat up my head if I didn't.

Okay. Here it is:

That's what I feel

Today I heard your voice after ages,
It felt the same again after so long,
I was yearning to hear your voice,
It felt as if I had got my life back.
Your voice had that soothing effect on me,
I was waiting for your call,
I couldn't call you.
I didn't have the strength to do so,
I just had my prayers to work,
Maybe God showed pity on me,
But it was a blessing for me, I swear.
The way you call my name,
It sends sparks in my body,
I don't know why,
I feel something different with you
I forget this world when I'm with you.

I guess that's why people say,

Love can happen only once,

And just with one person,

And I can only love you,

You and just you……………

I knew he would find it crazy but I waited for his verdict.

Wow! This is super awesome. You wrote this after your break up with Shashank, right? May be when you had a talk with him after a long time.

Yes.

I replied back.

You should write more and send it to newspapers and magazines.

Man, he was going bizarre. Getting this in print? He had certainly lost his mind, I was sure about it.

No way. Topic closed. No discussions please.

I somehow managed to close the topic.

No message since morning. Are you fine?

I saw his message while I was in the Metro, heading towards any home one evening.

Sorry, message card got over last night. I will get my voucher as soon as I reach home

Take care

I replied.

Ten minutes later my phone beeped only to find I had got my SMS pack. I knew it had to be Shashank.

What was the need for this? And how did you know I get the 88 INR SMS pack?

Got the info from net. And I can do this for a friend. I couldn't wait to talk to you, so thought of getting you the message card. Take it as your birthday gift

Eeek! No way. I want a better present.

Of course, I was kidding.

So, how was the day?

And our conversation continued. We had been chatting and messaging since long but we had never talked in person. Even though he had my number, he had never called me up till then.

Zakaas-The Food Joint, Phoenix Mall, Pune

"Di, I am so tense, I don't know what to do. Should I make this move?" A male voice echoed.

"According to what I have heard till now, I believe you should have a talk with her," a female voice replied.

"But I am scared. Will she agree?"

"I really can't comment on this. Most girls reject the first proposal; depends on what kind of an image you form in her heart and mind. Plus, you are at an advantage. You won't be there to get sandals in return if she gets annoyed at your proposal and you always have that useless Ritika to go back to," she said, laughing at him.

"Till now she has been helping me out with every problem that has come across in my relationship with Ritika. I just can't help falling for her."

"Do you know about her past properly?"

"Yes, she had a boyfriend but he called off the relation as he had got selected in NDA and he felt he couldn't let her suffer in the process but that was a long time back. She has already done her graduation. The wounds have healed; a shadow is all that remains."

"A shadow can also be frightful at times and it is always larger than the original size."

"From what I know, she has been single since long, but it's me who is going through a complex situation. I can't leave Ritika. That would be infidelity but I am falling for her no matter hard I try, her sweet face keeps coming to my mind. I read her messages for no rhyme or reason. She is the best girl for me."

"If you are pretty sure of your feelings, then go ahead but please leave Ritika once you embark on a journey with her. You say leaving Ritika would make you guilty; wouldn't staying with Ritika even after having the sweetest girl by your side be infidelity in your eyes? Wouldn't that make you guilty?"

"You are right Di, but when should I tell her all this?"

"Now."

"Now?" he asked in astonishment.

"It's now or never."

"Okay, I'll send her a message. If she is free, I will express my feelings right now."

A SURPRISE OR A SHOCK?

One day I received his message in the afternoon when my cell was on charging and I happened to miss it. It said: *Can you do me a favour?*

He had told me that his elder sister had come to his city, so he would be busy all day and that is why even I hadn't bothered to pick up my phone and check because Vishakha normally called on my landline. At around 8 p.m. I noticed I had four messages unread and all of them were from Shashank. And every message had the same content, the only difference was that they were sent at a time interval of one hour.

Yes... Sure. Anything wrong? I asked.

No. Can I call you up?

Yes.

My cell rang within a fraction of seconds.

"Hello," I heard him say. He had a sweet voice. It wasn't the masculine, excessively heavy voice but it was pleasing to ears.

"Hi! What happened, Shashsank? Is there any problem?" I asked.

"Not much. I wanted to say something."

"What?" I asked casually, not knowing an earthquake was about to come in my life.

"I love you."

What the fuck! Was this guy in his senses? Did he really say those three words to me?

"Shashank, are you alright?" I asked. Damn! What a stupid question to ask.

"Yes, I am perfectly fine. You must be thinking that I am crazy but I am not. I just couldn't help falling for you. The love and affection you showered on me, the care you have shown towards me is incomparable. Ritika never cared to know if I had had my breakfast, lunch or dinner. She never coaxed me to have food even if I didn't have but you were always present to talk to me, to cheer me up whenever I felt low. Even after being far, you are there to understand me closely."

"Shashank, I understand your feelings but this could be a case of infatuation. We have talked for the first time on the phone. You are hearing my voice for the first time and we have hardly been talking for seven months now. We haven't met face to face ever and there isn't any chance either. You don't know about my background, I don't know about yours and plus you are already in a relationship. For heaven's sake, remind yourself about Ritika," I blurted out.

"You don't need to remind me. I know about Ritika. I know she will leave me some day. She has never cared for me. The only problem I face is to get out of this relationship. Something stops me from doing the wrong thing and this is not infatuation. You have been in my thoughts for quite some time and I have been trying to make sure whether it's love or infatuation. And I know it is not infatuation. Got it?"

He had said it all in one go. I gulped some water and began to speak, "I respect your feelings, Shashank but I am certainly not ready to go into a relationship, neither with you nor with anyone else. I hope you are getting my point."

"Yes, I can understand. You can take your time, think over it and in case some day you feel I am good enough for you, I will be more than glad to have you as my angel."

"Okay, I will let you know but I hope this will not affect our friendship. I don't want it to get muddled up."

"No way would it ever happen and I want the same assurance from your side."

"Yes Sir. Anyway, I have to go now. Catch you later. Bye."

"Bye!"

❖ ❖ ❖

"Don't tell me that Shashank proposed to you!" Vishakha asked with her eyes popping out with surprise.

"As a matter of fact he did."

"Wow! This guy really has some guts. You hardly know each other and he is already committed to someone else but still he has the courage to ask you out. My God!"

"Shut up! Stop repeating this thing again and again. What is wrong with boys these days? They can propose to any girl without even giving a second thought."

"At least he is honest, Priyanka."

"Now where does honesty come from? We thought Dumbo to be honest too. I know he is a great guy, well natured and a good friend but this is it. The end comes here itself. I can't be getting into another trap."

"Stop talking to him then. Finish the story," Vishakha retorted.

"I can't. I have promised him."

"Promises are meant to be broken."

"I wish it was as easy to follow," I sighed.

Yes, it wasn't that easy to break the promise and that is because I happened to be an emotional fool and he is such a goody, goody fellow that you wouldn't like to hurt him. There was a little change in his behaviour after that day. For example, earlier it used to be 'good morning' but now it became 'good morning, my angel' and I was like who is this angel by the way? Me? Why?

Well, the reason he gave me blew me off. "It is because you gave me a second life, a rebirth in this life itself. You have brought back the colours of my life. Life was dull without you but now everything seems so beautiful." I liked the honesty in his words and felt great to have made a poor boy smile. It always feels good when you get to know that you are the reason behind someone's smile. Collars up! I deserved it, right.

Earlier it was just messaging, but now we did less of messaging and more of talking. He used to call in the afternoon to remind me of lunch even though he knew that the first thing I did after coming from NIFT was to eat. Hungry me! But he had this habit and I was kind of habitual to it now. In fact I felt awkward if he didn't call me or message me to remind about it. Before proposing, he would normally leave a message on now things were different.

"Hey, how are you?" he would ask every time he would call, even though we would be connected for half the day.

"Good, you tell"

"All well. So how was the day?"

And the moment he would ask this, I would start jabbering away. During the initial days of our talk, he had once remarked, "You talk very less." I am sure he would have eaten his words by now.

Every day he used to call me up telling me how his day passed, how nervous he was about the placement drive, what he liked and what he disliked, his friends and room mate. In a span of two months I had come to know everything about him. His family was his priority and even after being a final year student of engineering and staying away from home for the past three and a half years, he missed home. I would find him at home every fortnight. He would fight with his brother all day but he would never forget to give him a call each day, even if it meant more of fighting. I knew he loved blue and hated green. He loved chicken curry but hated cottage cheese. He loved all kinds of sweets but hated chocolate. Can you think about it? He hated chocolate. Why on earth did he do so? He liked strawberry ice cream and he knew I hated it. I loved being loyal to my chocolate. He had made me listen to so much of Eminem, even though I just didn't like it.

It was getting a little tough to be stuck on phone all day because I had a detective bro who would never let me be free.

"I can see you are getting quite busy these days. Who is the guy you have been talking to?"

"That's none of your business, got it?"

"Oooo! So you finally have a boyfriend? " he said.

"Nope. He is just a friend."

"Oooo! Loser boy, he talks to you daily and still couldn't make you his girlfriend. Sad!" he said, singing away, giving different frequencies to his thoughts.

"Look, stop all this. Okay? I am not interested in making a boyfriend or anything. You stay happy with your girlfriend, okay!"

"Huh! At least I have one and he doesn't. And mind you, I am going to break his muscles even if he tries to come close to you," he said clasping his right wrist in his left palm with his teeth tightly stuck, showing his angry face.

"You are still a kid and you should remain one. Got it?" I replied.

He gave me a disgusting look and went away.

It had been long since we had talked and I hadn't told him about the truth of my life even till now. I had started feeling guilty about this for quite some time now because he seemed to be coming closer to me. He was still with Ritika but he didn't bother about her calls any more. He had once said, "I know she will leave me one day or the other. She doesn't love me. This relation is a compromise for her. I wish I could let her off from this bond but I find it difficult. She was my first love and first love is always special, even if there are bitter endings. Life goes on like this. Thankfully I have you by my side. You have given me everything I have yearned for. I feel I am lucky to have you. I know it will be tough for you to accept me with a past like this, but I am glad you have been your true self."

"I know the pain of parting from a relation, so I will never force you to leave Ritika until she does." Saying this, I had changed the topic for it made me feel that I wasn't true to him. He was still unaware of the truth. He didn't know about my past, my true past, the ugly past that didn't let me go to him. It had been making me go crazy. And I really don't know why, but I couldn't find the right moment to tell him. Every time I wanted to say it, I would feel I shouldn't as it would hurt him. But one day, the truth had to be told to him.

AS LONG AS YOU LOVE ME

Shashank had been going berserk over the placement drives that were to arrive in his campus soon. He had been working on aptitudes, communication skills, brushing up his technical skills and what not. All day he used to do this. He went to college for his training sessions, came back and studied, studied and studied. He was working hard at it, really hard! He had been going restless and panicky too. Our talks became a little less and I realised I missed him a lot. Whenever we talked, he would ask, "Would I get selected? Do I stand anywhere?"

"Yes, you will. I know and I have faith in you," was all I would say to him. There was a lot more I wanted to tell him, to let him know that I would always stay by his side even if he didn't get selected. But the biggest problem with me was that I was never able to express what I feel exactly.

Frankly speaking, I didn't care about my status any more. I had nothing to lose or gain either. If I lost him, he would be just another guy like Shashank and Vishal but if I got him, I would be lucky indeed. I knew I was being unreasonable, talking to a guy whom I didn't know much and hadn't seen apart from Facebook. But there are certain things in life that hold no reason at all. And this time I needed a hell lot of support. Shashank had become my pillar of strength as he had helped me cope up with the shock I had got and I was definitely indebted to him for this. I was drawing closer to him day by day. His thoughts, his talks, his care, all were making me go crazy for him. But something was holding me back, my past which he was unaware of.

The night before his placement drive, he said to me, “Tomorrow I will know if my hard work of three years has paid off or not. In the past three years, all I had concentrated on was my studies. And if I get placed here, I can rest assured that I can buy you a living. Once I have this job in hand, I can try for IES and GATE too. I want this fourth and last year of my college to be spent with you. I want my life to make a new and fresh beginning with you. And I promise I will work hard to give you the kind of life your Dad gives you. You can take your own time but believe me, if some day you feel you need someone, you know where to find me.”

I was touched; any girl would be. Yes, I was a sucker for emotions. I don't why I was teary-eyed then. May be because I was way too tired of carrying the sadness in my life all by myself, maybe I needed some emotional support, maybe after a long time I deserved true happiness in life. It felt good to know that there was a person miles apart who cared about me and most essentially he gives a thought to our future.

Life gets so unpredictable at times. Vishal was so close to me, that we used to meet every day, yet his talks never made an impact on me or in any case he had never said such a thing to me, but there was Shashank who stayed far off, but had the courage to say this. Perhaps it was time to tell the truth to the man who wanted to make me happy. My cries grew harder and he became alert.

"What happened, Priyanka? I am sorry if I hurt you," he said with deep concern.

"No Shashank, you didn't. You are the sweetest guy I have ever met. I have to tell you something; something really important but I don't think it's the right time. Prepare well for your interview tomorrow. All the best! I should hang up now," I said in one go. I couldn't control my tears. They were tears of joy, tears of a newfound happiness.

"No, you don't have to. I want to know it. You can't deny me something. Whatever you have to say, say it now," he said softly but in a firm tone.

"Shashank, try to understand, it will hamper your performance tomorrow. Go to sleep," I said with a few sniffs and sobs in between, trying hard to convince him.

"I want to hear, right now. And I promise you, nothing can create an obstacle in my interview tomorrow. And luck also matters, so you don't have to think about it. Just tell me," he said authoritatively.

"Shashank, I have lied to you."

"How?"

"Umm…my story of Shashank, I mean my ex, it isn't true. There is lot to the story, a lot more than you know. It might separate us. And it will take a whole night to tell you my story," I told him with a quivering tone.

"I am all ears. Start now. We have the whole night."

"It happened when I was in the last year of my school..." I began with my story, crying at times in the middle.

He listened patiently to me giving small 'hmmm' and 'that's okay' responses. I rattled on for two- and- a- half hours. After I was done, he said, "Now get up and have water."

"I don't want to," I replied. I had cried a lot that night after ages. I was tired of crying and I didn't want any more tears in my life. But telling him everything made me feel lighter. I felt as if a mass of pain and dejection had fallen off my shoulders.

"Do as I say Priyanka."

I did as he said. I felt better after taking in some aqua.

Before I could say anything, I heard some music.

Although loneliness has always been a friend of mine

I'm leavin' my life in your hands.

People say I'm crazy and that I am blind

Risking it all in a glance,

And how you got me blind is still a mystery

I can't get you out of my head.

Don't care what is written in your history

As long as you're here with me.

I don't care who you are

Where you're from,

What you did,

As long as you love me,

Who you are where you're from

Don't care what you did.

As long as you love me.

Yes, it was Backstreet boys. He had said it all in one song. That was how Shashank made himself stand out of everyone else. He did the ordinary thing in an extraordinary way. I was happy that he had been so supportive.

"Thanks Shashank. I wonder how can two people with the same name be so different?" I said thoughtfully.

"Priyanka, we can't do anything about people. All you have to do is forgive and forget. Shashank can't be blamed. He was also in school that time and such things do happen and as for Vishal, you have to thank him for he supported you as a true friend when you needed him. So just forget your past and welcome the present with open arms. Don't think about it any more. And my opinion or feelings haven't changed even now. I loved you before and I love you even now. Now just relax, wish me luck and go to sleep," he said calmly. I was amazed to see that he didn't show signs of shock anywhere. He would have never expected this out of me but I was glad that he had taken it in a healthy manner.

"I am glad I have you with me, Shashank. Thanks for being there. Give your best tomorrow. I'll pray for you," I said with true feelings, promising myself that I would end my fight with God for him.

"Thank you, my angel. Good night and sweet dreams." I loved the way he called me angel.

"Good night, Shashank."

I slept peacefully finally. The burden of not telling him the truth had fallen down.

❖ ❖ ❖

I woke up early to wish for his interview. He was nervous. This was going to be his first one. It was obvious to be tense and I tried my best to keeps his fears off. After some time, I saw a card kept on my table that said 'To the best sis, Love you loads.' I was touched but how on earth did my bro make this for me? I mean there isn't even a single moment when we don't quarrel but this wasn't Sister's Day for sure. I searched every room, looking for him but he couldn't be found. Finally, I went to the terrace and saw him drinking his favourite black coffee. He turned around to find me and smiled.

"Good morning my sweetu bro. Loved the card you made for me but what's the occasion?" I said ruffling his hair.

"I am sorry Di," he said with head bent low.

"For what?" I asked puzzled.

"I need to apologise for being rude to you on numerous occasions. I didn't know my sis was going through so much of pain all alone."

I was still clueless as to what he was trying to convey and my face showed that in every way.

"Last night I heard everything," he said sheepishly.

"What? How? I mean you sleep like an ass every day," I said with my mouth wide open. How could he hear to my conversation with Shashank? This was seriously one hell of a situation, being caught talking to a guy late at night and who in the future might be your boyfriend is one of the most embarrassing condition for a girl.

"I do. But tomorrow when I woke up to pee, I heard you talking to someone. I knew you were facing the other side, so you wouldn't have seen me crawl from my bed. I heard you sobbing, so stopped by to listen to your conversation. I couldn't sleep all night thinking about this. And the person who was on other side of the person seems to be a nice person. Who was it?" he asked, smiling at me.

"He was Shashank, Shashank Mittal..." and I began with another story of the day.

My bro had grown big. He certainly had. He had begun to understand matters and analyse them in a mature way. Till now I knew he would make our family proud through his academics but now I knew he would make us proud by being a good human being too. That day I prayed. I prayed after an era. It felt good.

God, I know I haven't acknowledged you for giving me a pleasant life since long. I have been angry, but today I want a small gift from you. Please give him the happiness he deserves and I will do my best in every way to give him what he wants.

When I was done with my first class of the day at my institute, I received a message from Shashank telling me that his Aptitude Test was over and he had cleared it. I wanted to call him up but couldn't. So I messaged him, *That's great news. I know you will clear the HR too. All the best. <Hugs>*

I was happy about him and made a small prayer to God, thanking him for clearing his test and asking Him to get him selected too.

When he called me up in the evening, the first thing I wanted to ask him was whether he got it or not. But I was afraid because if in case the answer was negative, it would have made both of us sadder.

"Hey!" he spoke. His voice wasn't sounding cheerful. I thought he didn't get into it.

"Hi! How was the day?" I asked.

"It was fine. I have decided that I am not sitting for any more of these placement drives," he said sulkily.

"But why? Don't get disheartened. Everything happens for a reason. May be you deserve a better job. You will get next time for sure," I tried to sour d philosophical.

"I don't need to do that now, my angel. I have been selected" he said laughing hard. His happiness was reflected in his voice. Yes, he did it. He got selected in Bosch.

"Wow! Congrats. I am so happy for you. Time to party. Where's my treat?" I said sounding equally happy for him. Even though my happiness had no limits that day I couldn't express it the proper way. It almost felt that I was going through the best moment of my life.

"Ah! I wish I had you with me today. Anyway, I will party with friends and there is some good news. I am not telling about it now because I am still confused if it is really good for you or not."

"What? Did you leave Ritika?" I said laughing and stopped instantly as I realised I shouldn't have said this. I had no right to say this. But why did I say this? Did her presence really matter to me? Did she make me feel jealous?

"No, not that. There is something else. I will tell you after two days." He hung up the call after this.

Meanwhile I ran into Abhilash again. He was sitting at some food joint. But there was a girl with him and whose back faced me and they were having a drink from one glass. I don't know why but the girl looked a lot like Vishakha. I went closer to them without letting them know I was there. Oh! Yes, the cunning woman was here. She was holding his hand and smiling. So her latest prey was Abhilash. God, save him. I observed them for long and when I couldn't control myself, I boomed into them. I could tell you from their facial expressions that they had got the shock of their life.

"So Mr. Abhilash, how does it feel to date my best friend?" I said with a chuckle.

He blushed when I said this and Oh! My God, did I see my friend turn red too. My eyes went wide open when I saw Vish, the Vishakha get red with shyness. This was epic, truly epic. A moment to capture for sure.

"What is going on between you guys? You guys are going around and you didn't even tell me. Abhilash, I expect this from Vish, but not from you. I am highly disappointed," I said, making a frown.

"Priyanka, we wanted to give you some big news, rather very big news," Abhilash stopped while looking at Vishakha. She nodded in approval.

Wait a second. Did I just see a ring in Vish's ring finger. This was going be a breaking news, I was sure. I was shocked for I never thought Vish would fall in true love so soon. It had been like this since long. May be, it was time to grow up.

"Are you guys planning to get married or something?" I asked.

"Yeah..something like that. Not now but after she completes her post graduation. By then I will also be stable enough. It happened all of a sudden. I never thought we could fall in love but it happened and I am so glad I have her by my side."

"This calls for a celebration, guys. Let's party," I shouted aloud.

I made them cut a cute heart shaped cake and then we went to fill our stomachs with some real delicious food. I was surprised to see Vishakha decline to drink beer. Could a guy bring so many changes in a girl life ?

When we were alone, I asked Vishakha, "You are really serious about it, na?"

"Yes, definitely. I love him. I don't know how I fell in love with him but since then, life hasn't been as it used to be. I have dated all kinds of men, better than Abhi but the connection that I share with him is magical. He makes my life perfect. We are like perfectly perfect for each other," she said smiling at me.

"I am so happy for you. Does aunty know about him?"

"Yes, I told her yesterday. Abhi is taking Mom and me for lunch tomorrow. I can't wait to get married to him. Someone has truly said that love makes your life wonderful. It's like heaven on earth."

I smiled at her. How life had changed all of a sudden? Vish had got the love of her life and she was planning to get married even.

There was a time when we used to play with dolls together, getting them married to another and now one of us was going to get married. Time had surely flown by. Sweet memories of the past flitted across my eyes, our school life from kindergarten to XII and graduation. We had shared each and every moment together, happiness, joy, sorrow, fun, all of them had crossed our way and we had faced them collectively.

"How is Shashank?" Vishakha asked me waking me up from my thoughts.

"He is fine, got selected in Bosch, great package. What else could he ask for?" I replied.

"May be you," she said, smiling knowingly at me.

"What?" I asked.

"Yes, he has been patient with you for long. Don't you think so?" she answered and threw another question at me.

"Yes, you are right. He is a nice guy but I haven't even met him. All this makes me feel apprehensive," I said, sharing my concern with her.

"Take your time. You have to be wise in taking decisions for life," she replied, squeezing my hand in support.

DELHI HEIGHTS

"Guess what?" I excitedly asked Shashank.

"What?"

"Vish got engaged. She will be getting married after completing her PG. I am so happy," I kept dancing in the room while I told him this.

"Great news. Wish her congrats from my side," he said.

"Sure. Anyway what good news did you want to give me?" I asked.

"I am coming to Delhi," he said.

"What? When?" I was totally taken by surprise.

"I expected a better response," he said.

"Oh! Of course I am happy. Any specific reason for coming to Delhi? Where are you going to stay?" I asked.

"Yes. The reason is the lady I am talking to. I can't control myself from having a glimpse of my angel. And don't worry about accommodation. I will be staying with a friend. He is doing his coaching at Delhi and would be coming to pick me up."

I smiled when I got to know the reason. I asked, "So when are you coming?" An unknown shyness had engulfed me.

"Tomorrow night. Does the lady have time to meet me day after tomorrow morning? As for the venue, it has to be decided by you. And don't forget to make me meet your friends and if possible, your family too."

"Sure. I will be waiting for you," I replied as another night got lost in the sweet realisation of love.

That night was different. I kept on thinking how it would be to meet him in person. Would I be able to recognise him? Would he like me? How would I talk to him? Yes, I had fallen for him but the existence of Ritika haunted me day and night.

As soon as I woke up in the morning, I called up Vishakha to give her this news. She grew excited and we headed for a shopping spree. I got a blue off shoulder top with white jeggings. Thankfully, we got the stilettos with the same coloured top. A few accessories and we were done. Of course it took us a whole day to shop for all these items. Getting a good pair of clothes is easy, but getting accessories accordingly is tough. The only thing remaining was a gift for Shashank. We thought and thought and finally I got a card and a personalised coffee mug for him. Vish said that in this way he would always be reminded of me every time he drank coffee, plus, his day would always begin by being closer to me. I quite liked her thought. He called me up in the day to tell me that he had left Pune for New Delhi and would be meeting me the next day. All this increased my heart beats.

"Relax Priyanka, it's going to be just another date," Abhilash said to me while having lunch.

He had come to accompany us for lunch as he wanted to see his Vishakha.

"I don't know why but this date is making me a little nervous," I confessed.

"Admit it, you love him and you can't find a better man than him just the way Vishakha can't find a better man than me," he said, grinning hard.

"Very funny," I replied with Vish laughing in the background.

"Where does his friend stay?" Abhilash asked.

"I don't remember exactly. I guess somewhere in Laxmi Nagar. He is preparing for some competitive exam or something," I replied.

"Ah! Yes, that's the student area. Don't worry, I will pick him up and you guys can use my car for the day."

He was going out of the way to help me and I was really happy that Vish had made the right choice.

"At your service, Ma'am," Abhi said, handing over his car keys to me. Shashank now stood next to me and I seriously didn't know how to react. I hadn't looked at him till now. All I could see was he was very tall, almost six feet.

"Thank you," I said and Abhi took leave.

I sat in the driver's seat and Shashank spoke for the first time, "Let me drive."

"I stay here, so let me drive. You can drive when I come to your place," I said, adjusting my seat belt.

I could see him smile as I noticed from the corner of my eyes. My hands trembled while I drove. They had turned quite sweaty. We didn't talk much during the drive except for asking how the journey was and if he liked Delhi or not.

When we reached the parking lot of Select City Walk, I handed over the driver's position to him as I always had a problem in getting the car parked properly. As soon as I was getting out of the car, he held my hand and I turned around to see him looking at me, "Ah! Finally I got a close look at the angel who gave me another life."

I smiled back shyly. I looked at him closely. He was clean shaved and there was a small cut near his chin which might have formed due to shaving. The small pimple mark on his right cheek looked cute. Specs made him look decent and studious too. Some people look better with specs and Shashank was one of them.

We walked together to Barista. We began talking. We talked a lot, from anything to everything. I knew he didn't like chocolate brownies, but he ordered them for me. He even ate it. I fed him with my hand and he loved that for he didn't even try to pick up any piece with his hands after that. It was tough to look into each other's eyes but after three hours, it became okay.

While having lunch together, he held my hand. I withdrew it. I didn't want to, but I did. We had lunch in the same plate, our favourite butter chicken. While we were roaming about, he tried to touch my hand again and I let him do.

"You are looking beautiful," he whispered in my ears. I smiled back again.

In the meanwhile, I heard *'As long as you love me'* being played on the piano in the mall.

"This one is for you, my angel," and he said grabbed my hand to take me inside. I could see a cake, red roses, chocolates and a beautifully decorated hall." He gave me his hand and I took it. Soon there was the song I had always wanted my man to sing for me.

Would you dance, if I asked you to dance?

Would you run, and never look back?

Would you cry, if you saw me crying?

And would you save my soul, tonight?

Would you tremble, if I touched your lips?

Would you laugh? Oh please tell me this

Now would you die, for the one you love?

Hold me in your arms, tonight.

I had tears in my eyes. We cut the cake together and I walked proudly with the roses and chocolates. I had got the man of my life and this time I was sure he wouldn't leave me. But there was one obstacle Ritika. I didn't want to spoil my mood by thinking about her anyway now.

"How did you get all this arranged so fast?" I asked, while we were returning back.

"All thanks to Abhilash. He got things arranged for me at superfast speed. Without him, all this couldn't have been possible. Where are we going now?"

"To meet my bro, Tanishq."

"Wow! He agreed?" Shashank asked, getting excited.

"Yes, I had explained to him everything last night and he was more than happy to do the needful. He is super excited to meet you."

"So am I. I hope brother-in-law approves of me," he said mischievously but somewhere deep down, it felt good to hear this. An unknown feeling of shyness wrapped me on hearing this.

Tanishq was already waiting for us at GIP when we reached. "Why do you always have to be late?" he grumbled.

"I am sorry. I want you to meet Shashank," I said and got out of the crime of being late.

"Hey handsome boy, nice meeting you. You seem to have swept my sister off her feet," he said shaking hands with him.

They gelled together but there was some private chat that Tanishq had with Shashank which I knew not as I was asked not to poke my nose in matters of men. I know that was rude enough. They even had that guy hugs. What the hell was going on!

I had finally become committed again. This was different but it felt nice to have a man like Shashank. But long distance relations weren't easy.

"When is your train?" I asked, feeling sad that he was going away.

"Tonight, 11 p.m." he replied. Even he was feeling bad about it, I could sense.

"Can you not stay for one more day?" I asked, making a sad face with my eyes getting wet.

"I do want to. Never mind, I will stay back for a day. If I don't get reservation, I will catch a bus. I can't see my angel sad. My love wants me to stay back and I shall do anything for her," he said and I almost felt like kissing him, but refrained.

"I will ask Abhilash for help. And thank you so much for the wonderful day, Shashank," I said. We were sitting in the car ten steps away from Abhi's home. It was time to return Abhi's car.

Somehow it felt good to be with him alone in the car. We looked at each other closely and soon I closed my eyes. I knew a kiss was in demand but I was taken by surprise. He planted a kiss on my forehead and that's all. I had thought he would at least kiss me on my cheeks, if not lips. We drove further to Abhi's home. That night, sleep didn't come at all.

Another morning, another date and another panic attack. "Vishakhaaaaa!" I shouted on phone.

"Wear your white dress with the white ballerinas you bought last weekend. Don't disturb my sleep. We will catch up with you guys in the afternoon." Saying this, she hung up.

But I loved her. She knew I would call her up for this and without even saying, she told me what to wear. This is how a girlfriend comes handy and this is what we call heart to heart connection.

I took extra time to bathe, woke up even before Mom. I opened my wardrobe carefully, wore the white one-piece, white ballerina, white flower clip on my hair, a few curls. While curling them, I burnt my finger. My brother ran down to bring ice. I applied kohl, eyeliner, loads of mascara and lip gloss. I was done but oh God! Where was my white clutch bag. And the search began. After half an hour, I finally found it stuffed between my stoles in the shelf.

He called me up, saying that he was already waiting for me at Sector-15 Metro station. Tanishq asked me to hurry up and told me he would tell Mom that I had an early class at the institute. I almost ran across the road. Coincidentally he was also wearing white. Rugged blue denims with a white linen shirt looked fab on him. Folded sleeves and his metallic watch suited him perfectly well. I felt as if I was looking too bad paired with him. He held my hand as we walked to catch the Metro.

We went to India Gate and Lotus temple together. I don't know why on earth we went there when I had been there innumerable times but both these places have been special for me since long. I had spent a lot of time at Lotus temple, silently reminiscing about the past and the present. I found a different kind of peace there. As for India Gate, I hung out with friends there quite often, so had to take him there.

"How do you manage to look so beautiful?" he asked me all of a sudden.

"Someone's presence has made it happen today," I said, giving a witty reply.

"Priyanka, don't you want to know about my background? I mean now you have finally decided to stay with me, you should know a few things," he said seriously.

"I know that you have your Mom, Dad and an elder sister in your family. Di did her MBA from IBS, Hyderabad and recently shifted to Pune for her job. What else?" I said smilingly. Honestly speaking, all these things didn't matter to me. When you love a person you are not concerned with his financial or family background, but marriage demanded all this, apart from love. And that's why I hated the arranged-marriage system. I was capable enough to get myself bread and butter, so why look into how much the groom's party was able to produce every month?

"My Dad is a Bank Manager in SBI and my Mom is a homemaker. We are not as wealthy as you. My home is half as big as yours. Bhopal isn't as big as Delhi or Noida. One day or the other you will have to come to our place and it won't be as happening there as it is here. I will work very hard to reach up to that level. Plus, this is going to be a long-distance relationship. Will you be able to handle it? LDRs are tough to manage. I won't be able to meet you every time you would wish to but I can promise you I will come down to Delhi every two months," he said, sounding serious.

I smiled, held his hand tightly and said, "I know it will be tough but with you around, I will manage everything. Just be present to make me strong. I am okay with everything but what about Ritika? One day you will have to tell her everything or are you still waiting for her?" I asked, making my apprehensions clear.

"I wish I had an answer to this. I am not waiting for her but I just can't tell her to finish it off. It is becoming tough for me. I want to take my life forward with you but I need to clear the situation with her. I don't think I am that strong. I can't gather the guts to tell her all this."

I changed the topic for that moment. I didn't want to spoil my last day with Shashank. Vishakha, Abhilash, Shashank and I had lunch together. It was a great time spent together. After they left, he handed me something. On opening it, I found a most beautifully carved out pendant. It was nicely made in heart shape which gave it a classy, charming and sophisticated look. He took it in his hands and tied it around in my neck. There was a small 'S' and 'P' engraved on the heart with stones. It looked just perfect on me. The moment was perfect. We were very close to each other, I could smell his body odour. We came near and he gave a peck on my cheeks.

Finally the evening came and it was time to bid farewell. I escorted him to the railway station. I couldn't help it but there were tears in my eyes. He kissed them away. I held his hands tightly till it was time for the train to leave. I waved till I could see him. All I had with me was the pendant he had gifted me and his handkerchief through which he had wiped my tears few minutes back. Had I felt the same way for Vishal or Shashank Agrawal? Hell, no.

LONG-DISTANCE RELATIONSHIP

On reaching home, we returned to our daily routine of talking to each other all night and texting all day. He had been placed so even he became more relaxed. He had been talking to Ritika all this while. Sometimes it felt bad when I called him up at nine at night and his phone would be on call waiting, but I knew he would call after fifteen minutes because that was the maximum they talked.

His birthday was approaching and I was too confused about gifting him the best present. Vishakha and I had several discussions over it but all went futile. We just couldn't decide and then I remembered the last time he had come. He had kept on staring on a Rolex watch. I remembered the exact model. I went to the Rolex showroom to find out the cost. It was pretty high but I had saved enough all this while. I planned to take up a few extra orders so that I could easily get him the watch. Every day I worked overtime to add on the extra money needed and after a lot of pain and effort, I finally had the total amount.

I drove all the way excited to lay my hands on the watch. It had to be special. It was his first birthday with me. I had already told

Vishakha about it but some work had erupted all of a sudden and she couldn't be there to accompany me. I parked the car and in a hurry I left my cell phone in the car itself. I selected the piece and jumped happily at my achievement. I was almost dreaming how happy he would be on receiving my gift.

But when I returned back to my car, I saw something horrible. Thirty missed calls and all from Shashank. I grew worried and called him back instantly. But he rejected my call. I dialled and he rejected again. I tried three times but every time I got the same response. What on earth had happened? I sent him a message:

Left phone in the car, had some urgent work to complete.

I received a call in a few minutes. I was driving but I stopped it by the side of the road to pick up his call.

"What do you girls think of yourself?" he roared.

This was totally unexpected and I calmly replied, "I am sorry Shashank but I had an urgent work to do and in a hurry I left my cell phone in the car itself. And you normally don't call at this hour so I thought it wouldn't be that necessary even."

"Yes, that is what I get to listen whenever I call, whether it's you or Ritika. If I call her in the morning, she will give the same reason and so will you. I am a fool to fall for you girls. Bloody hell."

"Shashank, I really didn't want to disappoint you. I am sorry, this won't happen again, I promise. And you are no fool, you are the sweetest person in the whole world," I said, trying to calm him."

"Really?" he asked with an innocence of a kid.

"Yes, really. Now smile, baby."

"Yes sweetheart. I am sorry I shouted at you for no reason," he said softly.

"No problem. I can understand, it happens. You must be wanting to talk to me, *na*," I replied lovingly.

"Yes," he replied.

And thankfully the matter was solved. I felt like shooting Ritika that day.

❖ ❖ ❖

One day he asked me to book his tickets as his net wasn't working.

"Where are you planning to go?" I asked casually.

"I am going to meet Ritika."

The moment he said his, I went numb. What the hell! Why was he going to meet her now? I should have asked him the reason behind it, but I didn't. I had the right to but I didn't.

"Okay," was all I said.

"You must be thinking what a big bastard I am but I have this sudden urge to meet her. Even I don't know why. I had a talk with her regarding this. She agreed, unwillingly though."

"That's okay, I can understand. Send me the bank details, I will do it," I said and hung up.

I got his reservations done. He called back to confirm but I cut him short saying Mom wanted to see me. I walked to my room and as soon as I reached there, I cried. I cried for long. I cried till I got tired of crying. I don't remember when I slept while crying.

I did all my work according to the daily routine. In the afternoon I went to the Archies and got a happy birthday card for him. I packed the watch and the card and sent it to his address through courier. I had nothing to say to him. He had his duties toward Ritika and she was a step above me. I was the second woman, not she. I wanted to tell all this to Vishakha but I didn't. I remembered Madhuri Banerjee's quote from the book, *'Losing my Virginity and Other Dumb Ideas' that stated,* "Married men do not get a divorce. It is an urban myth." Was something like this going to happen with me too? No, I didn't want to be a victim of this situation.

I did talk normally to him every night even though the topic of Ritika had pierced my heart really hard. Soon his birthday came and I sent him three e-cards with lots of sweet messages in them. He had turned 22. I sent him 22 wishes and posted 22 cakes on his Facebook wall. By God's grace, my courier reached him on time. And he called me up in the afternoon, "Hey my Angel, I love you. I love you. I love you."

"Love you too, huuney" I replied.

"The watch is awesome. So you had seen me staring at it last time? There wasn't any need to spend all your money on this. Why do you love me so much?"

"Because I finally have the man who makes me complete," I answered with tears of joy.

"This is the best gift I have ever got in life. You are the best. The greeting card is awesome and the watch is stupendous. I have no words to describe how great I am feeling today."

"Thank you. I wish I could be there to see that happiness on your face. Now go and enjoy the party. Bye! Love you loads," I said, lest he kept his friends waiting.

"Yes Ma'am. Love you too. Bye!"

❖ ❖ ❖

Shashank says :

How can I be so ruthless to her? She has been the best to me and this is what I give her in return. She spent all her money to get me what I wished for and I am a coward to not grant her the position she deserves. She loves me wholeheartedly, I know. Even if she doesn't show at times, she does get hurt. She has been through a lot of bad times and I don't want her to go through them anymore. I wish I could give her everything she wanted. I might seem characterless to you, philandering around with two girls at the same time but I can't explain it. I so want things to be straight, but life doesn't seem to be straight all the time.

Why me? Why am I in love with two girls at the same time? I love Priyanka but what about Ritika? She is my first love, a love that I could never make mine. I wish I could end this life and put an end to everything around but the thought of Priyanka stops me from doing so. I have to work hard for her. I want to give her the best of life. I love to see that smile on her face. When her hair is ruffled by the air, I feel like hiding in their warmth. I love it when she sits on my lap, telling me her stories. For a boy, it's the best feeling when you get to know she has tears of joy for you. I still can't forget her baby-like expressions when we ate chocolate together. I had hated chocolate all my life but loved it when she fed it to me. There are certain things that only a girl can do and Priyanka is that girl for me.

IT'S SIX MONTH ANNIVERSARY

We were nearing six months to our relationship and Shashank had promised to come to Delhi on the D-day. Life had become pretty happy. Vishakha and Abhilash seemed to be in their own world and I didn't disturb them either. Even though people say it is tough to manage a long-distance relationship but for us it hadn't been that tough, at least that is what I could say from my six-month experience. In fact I somehow found the long-distance relation quite practical. You can talk to each other every night and concentrate on your work also. And a date every two months made it just perfect. I see couples cribbing over the fact that they are not able to meet like others but isn't the excitement of meeting and planning for a date every two month a different experience all together? The spice and enthusiasm of a date remains intact in LDR. You fight less and you have an easy life. No one is going to stop you from going out with anyone or staying up till wee hours of the morning. If you want to see each other, technology has advanced enough. You always have Skype, Yahoo and GTalk at your service. Life was fun overall.

"Hey!" he called me up one sunny afternoon.

"Yes sweetheart, what's up?" I asked.

"I called you to inform that I have got my reservations done and I will be reaching on 13th of December and leave on 15th. Stay ready for me. I'll be there to catch hold of my beautiful angel very soon," he informed.

"Wow! I am so happy," I squeaked in excitement.

"So am I. I have to go now. Catch you later."

This was going to be one great celebration. I would be roaming about with him for almost three days. I went to my daydreaming mode and when I woke up, I saw the calendar. I had just one week to finalise everything. I would be required to wind up my work at the store, I had to go shopping and the biggest task was to make Vish come along with me. Since the time she had got committed to Abhi, they had got stuck like glue to each other. This inseparable couple did form my life but for now I just needed his wife. Panic! Panic! Calm down, Priyanka, everything will be fine. I gulped some water and pressed my panic button. Who else other than Vishakha?

As I told her, she became excited and took Abhi in conference. Both of them teased me to the core. Abhi promised me his car for three days and directed Vish to help me out with shopping and deciding on gifts. So out we went, grabbing everything that came our way.

Day 1: Ice blue jeans, white shirt, black overcoat, black boots, silver danglers. Yes this was going to give me a classy look. It was too cold in Delhi and I had to take utmost care to cover myself as I catch cold easily.

Day 2: Green embroidered *kurti* with peacock blue leggings and *Nagras* to make the look perfect. A few matching bangles and earrings completed the date on Day 2. I had no plans to wear *kurti* earlier but when I saw Vish purchasing some for herself, I got one for myself too. She told me Indian men loved their girls to be in ethnic outfit. And I guess she was right. She was more experienced.

Day 3: Now it was getting really tough on deciding what to wear. When it comes to deciding on dresses, it becomes very difficult for girls to cross out on one dress. You find nothing suitable in your wardrobe and I believe every girl goes berserk before her special date. I finally decided I wouldn't get anything new for Day 3. I planned to wear the blue coloured dress that Shashank had gifted me two months back. It was tough to answer Mom who on earth had sent the courier to me but I had made up things, saying that it was from a client as she wanted me to work on it again. Thank God, the courier had the sender's name as Karishma Mittal who happened to be Shashank's sister. My gladiators matched perfectly well with them.

I had decided I would wear the pendant Shashank had gifted me. It would make him feel good. In fact this was suggested to me by Vishakha and boy, she was always right. And we were finally done with my shopping. But there was something that was left and that was the toughest part, Shashank's gift. We thought, thought and thought but nothing came to our mind. I got a wallet for him but the gift had to be something special. It would be marking our six-month anniversary. With no more of ideas coming to my mind, I got a few pictures of us together printed and began working on a collage. I bought some handmade paper and some decoration pieces. I had to literally hide them while bringing them to my house. Mom would have definitely asked about it and I would have not been in a position to reply. I started working on it at night, when everyone had gone to sleep. While talking to Shashank, I worked on it with full dedication, bringing my creative juices into action. Every night I would work on it. I didn't sleep for three nights continuously. But the result did show and my hard work had paid off. I showed it to Vishakha, even though I didn't want to. I needed feedback and Vish was the closest friend with whom I was frank enough. My bro also got to have a look at it and his comment was, 'I wish I had a girlfriend like you.'

Finally it was 13th of December and I went to the railway station to pick him up. He had said he would come all by himself but I was in no mood to wait. I started off my car and reached ten minutes before the arrival of the train. It was six in the morning when I reached Hazrat Nizamuddin Station. Tanishq had come half way with me. He had said he would handle things at home, I need not worry. This was the advantage of having your sibling by your side. They might fight with you all day but at the end of the day, they are sure to support you.

It was terribly cold but everything seemed to have became numb. All I knew was Shashank would be here any moment. I checked my hair for the 'nth' time in the mirror. I was waiting in my car outside the station getting restless. I drank loads of water and jumped about in my car seat. Suddenly my phone rang. It was Shashank. He had arrived and was approaching towards the exit. I looked at myself for the last time. Kohl check. Eyeliner check. Lip gloss check. Earrings well in place. And I got out of the car so that he could catch me.

Yes there was my prince. He was coming towards me, his eyes trying to look for me. He was ruffling his hair, he had sported the rugged look with his jacket resting on his arms. Our eyes met and he waved at me. He came closer to me and we hugged. This time there was no hesitation between us. He snatched the keys from my hands and sat in the driver's seat. "You are not driving, you don't know the way," I said.

"I know. Google maps to my rescue," he said with a naughty smile. I had to give in.

"Where are we heading to?" he asked.

"Where in the morning can we go? Abhi has invited us for breakfast at eight," I told him.

"No problem, let's go for a drive," he said and increased the speed of my car.

It was definitely an awesome experience. From Delhi to Gurgaon, we drove and drove, chance by chance. It felt great to feed him chips while he drove. Thank God, I had stuffed my bag with enough eatables. At times he would bite my fingers naughtily and I was no better either. I had my full share of the prank. The funniest part was feeding each other some chocolate. He made my lips chocolaty; it was sensuous and fun too. While I drove, he would kiss me on my cheeks and all I could do was smile at him. I had never felt shy thinking about kisses and smooch but the moment he kissed me, made me blush. It felt sweet, sweeter than honey and our love seemed eternal.

At 8:30 a.m. we reached Abhi's home. He gave us a warm welcome and a yummy breakfast too. Shashank and Abhi shared quite a great equation. Even though both of them were from different fields, they talked business. Abhi was from finance field and Shashank had an engineering background, but they talked like anything. At that time I felt the absence of Vishakha. Thankfully she came at 9:15 a.m. when we were halfway through our breakfast. I was getting completely bored with their boyish talk, Vishakha came as a saviour. We finally bid them adieu.

We headed to GIP, Noida. Being a weekday, it was quite empty. We sat in one of the benches with our hands entangled in each other's. I lay my head on his shoulders and how time passed by we knew not. I checked my wristwatch, it was five in the evening. We had missed lunch and it didn't even feel like we had empty stomachs. We headed to Barista to have some coffee and he ordered chocolate brownies again. He kept staring at me for long and then said, "Kiss me."

"What?" I asked astonished.

"Yes, kiss me now" he said with a naughty grin.

"Shut up!" I gave him my reply laughing at him.

He made a face like a small kid and I felt like pulling his cheeks and I don't hesitate when I feel like doing something. I did pull his cheeks hard and so did he in return.

I reached home at eight when I saw Mom packing.

"Oh! You are back. How was the party at Vishakha's place? I am so happy for her. She is soon to get married. I hope you get a good man like her."

So Vishakha and Tanishq had already made up the story. Clever indeed!

"The party was awesome. By the way, where are you going?" I asked.

"Oh! I am sorry sweetheart but there is a wedding at a distant relative's place and we need to go there. Your Dad, Tanishq and me are going. Tanishq told me you have an important project to submit tomorrow, so I guess we will have to leave you here. Tai will be there to cook food for you or if you need any assistance. I have had a talk with Vishakha and she has agreed to come up to stay with you at night," she said in one tone as she packed up everything hurriedly.

Great, I thought. Mom and Dad left in half an hour and within a fraction of seconds, a thought came to my mind. Why not invite Shashank for breakfast at home? It would be great to cook for him. For a woman, it is actually a nice feeling to make food for her man. Love changes you so much and for good. The transformation is quite visible and worthy too. True love makes you do things which you find funny. You suddenly begin to start cooking for him and dressing up for him. You feel shy when he compliments you on your looks and you feel content that your effort has paid off. Of course, he will love you anyway. You love to know his response when he has the first bite of the delicacy prepared by you. And if a man is really in love, he will never complain or crib about it for he knows that his woman has put in a lot of effort into it just to see a smile on his face.

I thought of making vegetable sandwiches and omelette for breakfast, but there was something else that I especially wanted to make for him. A chocolate cake. I entered the kitchen, a territory where I didn't land in much. I searched through the place to find if all the items were present or not but as I was not aware where things were present, I headed to the local market to get all the stuff. I reached home at 9:15 p.m. with all the stuff. I was exhausted but called up Shashank to give the news. I had handed him a local SIM to use for his three-day stay and we used it to the hilt.

The next morning I woke up at five, even after sleeping at 3 a.m. Flour, cocoa powder, eggs, vanilla essence, sugar, butter, baking powder, milk, all in place. Yes I was ready to make a cake to celebrate our six-month anniversary. I had never thought our anniversary would go like this but it was happening. I pinched myself to feel if it was really happening. Ouch! It hurt. Yes, it was real. I had asked Shashank to come over to my place by eight or so. In an hour I was done with the cake preparation. Decoration took another half an hour. Time was running by. Oh God! Why didn't I call Vishakha for help? I worked super fast. He called me up at 7:45 to tell me that he was ready and about to leave. I gave him the directions to my home. The breakfast was prepared but I hadn't got ready by then. I rushed to the washroom, wore the outfit decided for the day and got ready. By the time I was done with setting up the table, I heard the bell ring.

I ran to open the door. Buster didn't even bark once when he saw Shashank come in. On the contrary, they shook hands. He had brought flowers for me; white, yellow and red roses. They were pretty and as usual he hadn't come without chocolates. I hugged him as he gave the flowers to me.

"You look gorgeous in wet hair."

I smiled and thanked him. I wondered when he would get tired of complimenting me. We entered together in my home. He looked around and said, "You have a wonderful mansion. My father-in-law is a rich man," he said as he jumped on the sofa

"Thank you," I said, smiling at him.

"One day even I will get you a house like this, I promise," he said and all I could do was smile again.

"You must be thirsty. Let me get you some water," I said running to the kitchen.

He drank some water and said, "Show me your house and I am dying to see your room, the place from where you talk to me."

I showed him my home, Mom and Dad's room, our study, Grandma's room when she comes to our place, Tanishq's room and finally we came to my room. He looked at the pictures hanging around in the room. There were my childhood pics at which we both laughed as we saw them. There was one in which I was sitting in the middle of the bed with lots of teddy bears and dolls around. He smiled while looking at it and said, "You look prettier than the dolls in the background."

There was a picture of Mom and Dad together in which Dad was holding Mom from behind. He took me in front of the mirror and hugged me just like Dad had done to Mom. We looked at each other and smiled. I blushed at his gesture.

"Don't you think we should have breakfast now? The food is getting cold," I suggested.

"Sure, I am starving."

We headed to the dining hall. I served him sandwiches and orange juice. While he ate, I peeled oranges for him. He made me eat breakfast and praised me for my culinary skill. "I am lucky to have a wife who is a good cook. My Mom will be happy to have you as her daughter-in-law," he said while he ate.

After breakfast, we sat together in my room, talking. I sat on his lap as I showed him photo albums of childhood. He heard everything attentively. I looked at the clock. It showed 11:30 a.m. I thought it was time to cut the cake. I asked him to close his eyes and tied a cloth around his eyes. I made him sit on the sofa and swiftly brought the cake out of the refrigerator. It looked yummy. 'For the man who completes me,' I had scribbled this on the cake. I lit two candles and untied the cloth. His eyes showed a warm surprise. He smiled lovingly at me and hugged me tightly. I don't know why, but his eyes were wet then. We clicked the pic of the cake and cut it together. I pasted the chocolate on his face and he did the some in return. We took a piece, half of it in my mouth and the rest in his. We smooched then and there. I presented him the collage I had made and the wallet. I gave a big piece of cake to Buster too. It happily ate and jumped for more. Shashank and Buster seemed to be getting on very well. I loved the sight.

We returned to my room. The weather outside was too cold and I took a blanket to cover myself. We sat too close to each other. He looked into my eyes. I could see the warmth of love in them.

"Why do you love me so much?" his eyes asked.

"Love has no reason," my eyes replied.

"I want us to be together forever," his eyes conveyed.

"Till eternity," I responded.

"We complete each other, right." He asked.

"Yes, I am incomplete without you," I answer.

I snuggled close to him, hiding in his arms. I could feel the warmth of his body. I could feel the heat within our bodies. Burning desires made us draw closer and closer till our lips locked. We kissed for how long I knew not. Soon I could feel his bare chest and his hands searching for the hook of my bra. Inhibitions flew out of the window and I was finally his woman; he was the man who completed me in a true sense. We lay satisfied in each other's arms and I don't remember when I slept off in the protection of his arms.

When I woke up, I saw him looking at me and smiling for no reason.

"What happened?" I asked.

"Nothing," he said, smiling at me and kissed me on my forehead.

It was five in the evening. I got up and we took a hot shower together. Both of us were hungry, but we had nothing to eat. We went to the kitchen and he made Maggi for both of us while I prepared coffee. We watched the movies 'A Walk to Remember' and '50 First Dates' while he fed me Maggi in my usual position of sitting on his lap. It was the most romantic part of the day.

Vishakha called in the evening, "Should I come over to your place or is Shashank stopping by?" she chuckled as she said this.

"Shut up! Come over to my place; no excuses, and stop teasing me."

"Okay, I will be there by eight," she replied as she hung up the call.

Shashank left at 8:30 p.m. when Vishakha reached my house. Her Mom had sent dinner for us, so there was no need to ask Tai to come over and prepare dinner.

"So how was the date? Did something?" she asked as she opened the refrigerator.

Oh No, there was the leftover cake.

"No we didn't. Just a smooch," I replied rather coolly. I didn't want her to know about it even though she was my best friend. I felt shy about telling about it.

"Oh my my. Someone seems to have baked a cake. Special anniversary cake," she said as she took her piece.

"Yes and it turned out to be pretty tasty," I said, smiling.

We had dinner and after that I had no energy left to talk to her. It was getting a little difficult to walk or sit as it hurt. Losing one's virginity to the man you love is surely the best thing in the world, but it does pain. So I preferred to sleep and slept like mad that night. I didn't feel like waking up in the morning but I had to. It was Shashank's last day in Delhi. We stopped by at the Metro station and talked there for a while before heading towards Saket. We went to Barista, the place where we had our first date. He handed me a gift. On unwrapping it, I found a teddy bear and an exquisite bracelet. Shashank's choice was truly commendable including me, don't you think so?

He had his flight that evening. Abhilash and Vishakha came to accompany him to the Airport. I was already in tears when we sat in the car. While on our way to Indira Gandhi Domestic Airport, I held his hands tightly. A tear dropped on his hands. He wiped my tears with his fingers and gave me his handkerchief. I wiped the rest. He looked into my eyes which said, 'Don't cry, baby. I will come soon'. I calmed myself and as he went towards the entry. I waved to him with a smile because I knew that it was difficult for him too.

I had asked him to inform me as soon as he reached Pune and by the time it was ten, I received his message telling me that his jet had just landed and he would reach home in an hour or so. He asked me to sleep as even he was tired. But I couldn't resist and called him instantly. While we were talking, his elder sister snatched his phone and began to speak, "Hi Priyanka. This is Karishma here" she squeaked in excitement.

I wasn't expecting her to be there but I replied with full enthusiasm, "Hi Di. How are you?"

"I am good. I hope you guys had great fun together," she said.

"Yes Di, we had an awesome time. All thanks to you. You arranged for the tickets at short notice."

"Anything for you, darling. The next time I come down to Delhi, we are meeting for sure and if this donkey teases you or irritates you let me know. I will thrash him up."

"Sure Di and do come soon. I am eager to meet you," I said.

"Same here. Now talk to him. I don't want to disturb the love birds," she said and laughed as she handed over the phone to Shashank. We talked for some time and I soon slept off.

When I woke up in the morning I saw his text: *Good morning, my angel. I hope it isn't hurting much now.*

I smiled as I read his message.

Good morning sweetheart and it isn't paining any more. Love you. Take care

I loved his concern. The last time I had fallen ill, he had called me a hundred times to check if I had medicines on time or visited to the doctor. We had turned quite open to each other in the past few days. And I could easily tell him now if I was going through my bad days and wouldn't be able to talk much. He would become extra caring about me during that time and would silently bear my mood swings.

LIFE DOESN'T COME WITH GUARANTEES

His semester was nearing and it was high time we stopped talking much. He started studying for hours together. He was soon to become a graduate. He would be a full-fledged engineer now. He had even secured a high score in GATE, enough to get him into some reputed college but he wanted to work first. We didn't realise how time flew by and he was soon donning the hat of a graduate. He called me up from Pune, telling me that he had scored well in his exams and this was the happiest moment of his life. He wanted me to be by his side.

"I said he was always there in my prayers and I would be sitting by his side for sure when he would receive the best employee of the year award."

But there was one thing that had still not gone out of our lives. Ritika. We didn't raise her topic deliberately. On the day of his convocation ceremony, he called me up, saying, "Ritika walked out of our relation last night, saying she couldn't take it further any more."

"What? And you are telling me now," I asked in disbelief. I didn't know whether I should be happy or sad.

"Yes, it's good for us but I some how feel bad. I mean I was in contact with her for long, even though she never made me feel like her partner. But I am feeling a void, a kind of uneasy feeling," he said.

I didn't know what to say, so I stayed silent. Our talks became less after that. I didn't know how to react or act upon. All I did was to stay by his side. I never opened the topic myself but he did miss her. He told me things about her, those that he had told me earlier and also those he hadn't. He was still loving towards me no doubt but the charm and spark in his voice was missing. I was feeling sad at the events, but I could hardly do anything about it.

❖ ❖ ❖

Gloria Jean's Coffee, Phoenix Mall, Pune

"Do you even know what you are doing to her?" a female voice seemed to say in an angry tone.

"What do you mean, Di?"

"You were going all around with her for so many months and you even crossed your limits. The girl gave her everything to you and you are stuck up with Ritika" the female was in no mood to control her anger.

"Di, I don't want to talk about it, please."

"And this is all I want to talk about," she retorted.

"Please, don't pester me for anything," the male voice replied.

"Ritika was your past, forget her. She didn't acknowledge you for anything. She was a whore, who was roaming about with some other guy while she dated you. What kind of a man are you? You are crying for a girl who never gave you the position you deserved and you are ignoring a girl who accepted you as you are. Wake up from your dreams,

Mr. Shashank Mittal. Come back to reality," she said shaking up her brother.

He stood up and began to walk silently. His sister didn't follow him back.

❖ ❖ ❖

It was four in the evening when I received a call from Shashank.

I picked it up and said, "Hello!"

"Can you meet me outside CSM in two hours?"

Was he nuts? Yes, that is what I thought.

"What? Are you crazy? Where are you?" I replied.

"I am at the airport. I will see you soon. Be there on time. I have something important to tell you," he said as he hung up.

What could be so important that he had arrived here all of a sudden? Was he here to break up everything? I thought as I closed my store. I took a shower and got dressed as fast as I could. My mind had lost its logic by that time and ugly thoughts crept into my mind while I combed my hair I went and stood at the Metro station waiting for the Metro to arrive. I had to reach Sector 18 and it had begun to rain by the time, I came out of the Metro station.

I saw Shashank coming from a distance. I stood still as I looked at him, completely lost. It had started to pour heavily but nothing mattered. I stood in the middle of the road. He soon came in front of me and knelt down with his head bowed down, "I seek your forgiveness, Master," he said.

I took his face in my hands and made him stand. He had tears in his eyes and so did I. My struggles had finally ended. He hugged me tightly and began to weep. Even though we had tears in our eyes, everyone out there began to cheer us! He with drew his hands from his pocket, trying to find something and slid it into my ring finger. I looked at the ring and Shashank. Words had ceased to express emotions that moment. He took my hands in his and we began to walk together. What better happy ending could I have asked for?

EPILOGUE

Don't you want to know what happened after that? Yes, we courted for four years. He got posted to Hyderabad, Bangalore, Mumbai, Indore and even Delhi, but nothing came in between our love. In between he got a chance to work in the US too. It was a tough period for us as we could no more indulge in meet every-two-month ritual, but we coped with everything.

Vishakha and Abhilash got married and my Mom wanted to see me in the bridal attire soon. We sat down to discuss our marriage with our parents. Dad did try to find flaws in him but there weren't any. Soon he became his best friend and I was married off to the man I had loved and devoted myself to.

We shifted to Pune after marriage. I opened a clothing line and soon got a hefty number of satisfied clients and customers to my credit. Three years later, one morning I told him, "Shashank, you are going to be Dad on our next marriage anniversary."

He took me in his arms and his joy knew no bounds. Our first son was born this January and we named him Shreyank. His eyes and nose look like his Dad, but everything else resembles me. Life has been great with Shashank and Shreyank around. We are planning to have another addition to our family by the next two years. And as for now, we are shifting to Texas as Shashank's company wants him there.

Life has come a full swing for me and I can thank God no less for the blessings he has showered on us. There are millions of people in this world and many cross our life but there is always one out of those millions who becomes the love of our life. If you love someone, love till the end. Love can happen anywhere; school, college, office or on social networking sites and it really doesn't matter where you meet. What matters is if you are true or not. I have always seen people say that love on Facebook is fake but then, we all know that the coin has two faces. If hundreds of guys and gals get ditched there, few of us like us get the love of our life too. I found betrayal in a relationship where I knew everything about the guy and found true love in person about whom I knew nothing. It's just a matter of luck and how true you remain to a relationship. Obstacles are bound to come but true love will overcome it anyhow. A little bit of support from your partner is all that does the best to your life. Who says long-distance relations aren't successful?

Uff Ye Emotions

(With Free Music Album)

A Collection of Award Winning Love Stories

Editor	:	Vinit K. Bansal
Publisher	:	Mahaveer Publishers
ISBN(10)	:	9350880385
ISBN(13)	:	9789350880388
MRP	:	₹ 139/-
Pages	:	208
Binding	:	Paperback
Category	:	Fiction/Romance

About the Book

Perhaps, emotions are the most beautiful things in the world which cannot be seen or even touched. Interestingly, they can only be felt with the heart. Love is the purest and primary among them with its various shades. We all have our own definitions of this magical word, but, its beyond explanation. It is always around us. The very existence of this beautiful universe is founded on love only.

Love has been the most talked about subject since ages and has always come to us through stories and became a part of us. Almost each of us has experienced the magic of this emotion in one form or other in our lives.

Uff Ye Emotions is trying to recapture the magic of love through 12 beautiful award winning stories which were selected after a nation-wide contest.

Stories in this anthology are soaked with intense emotions: Adoration, affection, love, friendship, fondness, attraction, caring, compassion, sentimentality, desire, lust, passion, longing, infatuation, envy, jealousy etc. which truly complete our lives. Love stories from diverse age groups, from different corners of the country and containing different shades of love.

Selected and edited by Vinit K. Bansal, this anthology will certainly enthrall readers and will make them feel the tenderness of this magical thing, called love.

Ten Shades of Life (Fablery)

Editor	:	Nethra A
Publisher	:	Mahaveer Publishers
ISBN(10)	:	9350880415
ISBN(13)	:	9789350880418
MRP	:	₹ 139/-
Pages	:	240
Binding	:	Paperback
Category	:	Fiction/Romance

About the Book

In times when anthologies dwell on prosaic romantic accounts, Fablery presents ten shades of life. From a nail-biting thriller to a spine-chilling ghost story, an exquisite romance to an ingenious fantasy, an adventurous science-fiction to mirthful and remarkable experiences of salaried men, stories of heroes and philosophies of life - it attends to the preferences of all readers.

When anthologies contain stories of one genre, after reading a couple of stories they get predictable and fail to keep a reader's interest until the end, but a multi-genre book has something to offer to everyone and many things to one reader.

The writing styles of all the writers whose stories are included in this book are grand and the plots so engaging that they will force you to read another page and one another before you finally close the book. The stories will take you on a roller coaster between reality and fiction.

The Lost Paradise

Author	:	Anjali Vaswani / Vikas Bansal
Publisher	:	Mahaveer Publishers
ISBN(10)	:	9350880520
ISBN(13)	:	9789350880524
MRP	:	₹ 139/-
Pages	:	168
Binding	:	Paperback
Category	:	Fiction/Romance

About the Book

Riya was in a dilemma. Should she help her hostel-friend Kamini, who was involved in a sex-and-drugs racket and was depending on her to get her out of the mess? Riya had always dreamt big of becoming a politician some day -- so this was her chance to really help out innocent girl-victims and bust a racket...

Or should she just concentrate on her studies and enjoy the attentions of her handsome boyfriend Vivaan with whom she soon planned to tie the knot?

More important, could she help Kamini without getting into really dangerous waters herself and risking her own life and the lives of all those whom she loved?

'Some love....' unravels the rare path taken by a gutsy, urban collegian and the repercussions it has on her life.

I Loved Too Much... He Loved Too Many!

Author	:	Shikha Sharma
Publisher	:	Mahaveer Publishers
ISBN(10)	:	9350880334
ISBN(13)	:	9789350880333
MRP	:	₹ 125/-
Pages	:	192
Binding	:	Paperback
Category	:	Fiction/Romance

About the Book

Love- isn't it something that all of us chase at some points in our lives?

When she said 'I love you', she meant it forever....

When he said 'I love you', even he meant it forever...

But is that enough for a happy ending?

But do love stories even end at all?

Love is a four lettered word, but so is lust... so how could one find the difference between the two?

How can one know that it is love this time and not just another relationship?

How can someone seek true love at the time when just a minor tiff results in changing of facebook status as 'complicated' or even 'single'?

Join Lavishka and Tanmay in the journey of their quest for love, their fulfillment of desires and their discovery of their inhibited self and unveil the answers.